Evie's heart was thrumming with excitement, trepidation and a little of something else. That something else—incredulity at her own behavior.

She felt as if she were part of some old film, dashing off around the world, traveling on an overnight sleeper train to Hong Kong from Shanghai, where she would take a boat out to Indonesia, following coordinates to who-knew-where.

The coordinates could be anything. They could be nothing. But she couldn't shake the feeling that she would find answers there. Answers to questions the professor had spent his life searching for. Answers to questions that had ruined her reputation? She didn't care too much for that. She had learned long ago that people would think what they thought about her and nothing she did would change that. Even tonight, with Mateo. He had decided that she was too fragile for him, too *innocent*.

A knock pounded against the door. She reached for the ticket and opened the door, only to step back in shock.

"What the hell do you think you're doing?"

Mateo Marin loomed impossibly large in the small doorway, still wearing the tuxedo from the auction earlier that evening.

Pippa Roscoe lives in Norfolk near her family and makes daily promises to herself that this is the day she'll leave the computer to take a long walk in the countryside. She can't remember a time when she wasn't dreaming about handsome heroes and innocent heroines. Totally her mother's fault, of course—she gave Pippa her first romance to read at the age of seven! She is inconceivably happy that she gets to share those daydreams with you all. Follow her on Twitter @pipparoscoe.

Books by Pippa Roscoe

Harlequin Presents

The Wife the Spaniard Never Forgot

A Billion-Dollar Revenge

Expecting Her Enemy's Heir

The Diamond Inheritance

Terms of Their Costa Rican Temptation
From One Night to Desert Queen
The Greek Secret She Carries

The Royals of Svardia

Snowbound with His Forbidden Princess
Stolen from Her Royal Wedding
Claimed to Save His Crown

Visit the Author Profile page
at Harlequin.com for more titles.

Pippa Roscoe

HIS JET-SET NIGHTS WITH THE INNOCENT

HARLEQUIN
PRESENTS

ISBN-13: 978-1-335-59291-0

His Jet-Set Nights with the Innocent

Copyright © 2023 by Pippa Roscoe

Recycling programs
for this product may
not exist in your area.

For questions and comments about the quality of this book,
please contact us at CustomerService@Harlequin.com.

Harlequin Enterprises ULC
22 Adelaide St. West, 41st Floor
Toronto, Ontario M5H 4E3, Canada
www.Harlequin.com

Printed in U.S.A.

HIS JET-SET NIGHTS
WITH THE INNOCENT

For anyone who grew up loving adventures, treasure hunts, pirate stories and romances as much as I did.

This one is for us.

(Any mistakes are very much my own.)

xx

CHAPTER ONE

IT WAS A surprise to many that Evie Edwards didn't *hate* the room she'd been assigned for her lectures. At the far end of the London campus, down the back stairs of the smallest building, along a corridor with less than fully functioning lights was a door to what looked like a store room, bearing the bold declaration of Lecture Room Four.

While the room was considered a lecture hall, there was nothing remotely academic about it. Not the rows of black plastic chairs placed awkwardly in a semi-circle around her chair, or the large A3 clipboard that looked more boardroom than school room. Part of the issue was that, much like her lecture hall, she just didn't *look* the part of the University of South-East London's Lecturer in Archaeology.

At the age of twenty-five, she was mistaken for being either a PhD student or a teaching assistant, which Evie could begrudgingly understand. She had never truly fitted in, having finished her A levels by the time she was sixteen and her degree by eighteen.

Her Masters rolled into her PhD at nineteen and she had passed her viva for her doctorate by twenty-one.

And with an IQ higher than one hundred and sixty Evie either failed to live up to anticipation or confounded those with lower expectations. Her adoptive parents, Carol and Alan, leaned towards the former, where mostly everyone else leaned into the latter.

'It doesn't matter what they think at the beginning, it's what they think at the end that counts.'

Professor Marin's words echoed through her mind and she felt the sting of his loss throb a little as a group of fresh-faced students filed into the room. But she buried it deep, knowing that, as the first lecture of the year for the new crop of undergraduates, *this* was Evie's only chance to grab and hold her students' attention. Positioning herself in the centre of the room, she took in the familiar sense of expectation, excitement and a little trepidation universal to all students on their first day. She counted heads and waited a few more minutes, aware of just how many students would come in late, having struggled to find Lecture Room Four in the back of beyond.

'Good morning,' she said in a bright, confident voice after the door closed behind the last few stragglers. 'Welcome to the BA Programme in Archaeology.' Evie's glance skimmed the faces of students who sat up a little taller, eyes a little wider, recognising her finally as their new professor. 'Archaeology is the study of the past, but from investigation of the material remains left throughout history we can see what it means to be human. In your first year, your modules will cover…'

Evie slipped into the rehearsed welcome, soothed by the familiar outline of the lecture programme she would give over the next year. This was her domain and she was happy here. It was comfortable, even if there was a sense of disappointment that muddied the waters.

As she was wrapping up, she ignored the door to the lecture hall that opened and closed, refusing to be knocked from her stride. Perhaps it was the Dean, come to deny her conference proposal request. Again. She'd spent the entire summer on it and knew its merits; it was excellent, but the Dean was wary of being tainted by the reputation that she had already earned herself in her four-year career. A reputation that would have been made precarious enough by her age and gender, but that had been damaged irrevocably by her work with Professor Marin and their research area. Stubbornness and loyalty steeled her spine, even now. She wouldn't take back her work and time with Prof for anyone or anything.

So, as the students filed past her on their way out of the room, she gathered her lecture materials and prepared herself for the overbearing obsequiousness of her boss. But when she turned round, she was so shocked she nearly dropped everything she was holding. Rather than the red-faced, sweaty visage of the Dean of USEL, a shockingly beautiful blonde-haired woman stood before her.

'Your Majesty,' Evie stated, somewhat obviously, to the Queen of Iondorra, immediately dropping into an awkward curtsy.

By the time Evie had straightened, she could just make out a few figures placed around the small lecture hall in shadows.

'Professor Edwards,' the Queen said with a perfect smile. 'It is nice to finally make your acquaintance.'

Evie nodded as if they'd had an arrangement to meet when she knew that they'd had nothing of the sort. She was as shocked by the sudden appearance of the ruler of the small European kingdom as she would have been had Cleopatra stepped right out of the pages of a history book.

Queen Sofia of Iondorra gestured towards the front row of seats and waited for Evie to sit down before taking a seat right beside her.

'So this is where they put a prominent professor whose thesis was focused on eighteenth-century Iondorran history?' she asked, looking around her and appearing somewhat dissatisfied.

Alarmed at the thought the Queen would take it as a slight against Iondorra, rather than what it was—a slight against her—Evie rushed to reassure the Queen that she liked teaching in this room, a reassurance which was gently waved away with the sweep of a gloved hand.

'I was sorry to hear of Professor Marin's passing,' Queen Sofia said. 'I know that we weren't able to acknowledge his theories publicly, but they were of interest to…my family.'

Evie looked down, unsure—as always—that it was for her to accept sympathies as if she were a family member. He had been family to her. Not on paper. But the professor had understood her, accepted her, in a way that not even Carol and Alan had. But every time she received condolences she couldn't help but remember the looming figure of the son who had barely made it to stand at the back of the graveyard where Professor Marin had been laid to rest. The son who had not spoken a word to his father in the three years before his passing. But before the well of a familiar resentment stirred, she brought her focus back to the Queen.

'Professor Edwards, I would like to talk to you about a very sensitive matter. A matter that, I'm afraid, would need the utmost secrecy and discretion, which is why, before I explain anything further, I would like you to sign a non-disclosure agreement.'

Queen Sofia held out her hand and a man appeared from the shadows with a sheaf of papers and a pen.

'Personally, I detest the things and I understand if you feel that you—'

'There is no need to explain, I'll happily sign the NDA.'

Evie missed the slight reddening of the assistant's cheeks from the way she had accidentally interrupted the Queen of Iondorra as she bent over the legally binding document and signed her name.

Evie might not know what was going on, but there was a heaviness about the woman who had once been known as the Widow Princess, before finding true love with a Greek billionaire. Theo Tersi had become the Queen's consort when her father, King Frederick, had stepped down and Princess Sofia had claimed the throne.

The Queen's assistant retrieved the document, placed his signature in what must have been the witness box, tore along the perforated edge of the paper and returned what looked like a bound thesis to her. Frowning, Evie scanned the blank cover, unable to resist running her hand over the royal insignia embossed into the thick red cartridge paper.

'I'm afraid we don't have much time,' Queen Sofia explained, 'so I have to be quite blunt. There is an item up for auction in Shanghai in three days. An item the vendor is claiming to have once belonged to the pirate Loriella Desaparecer.'

Evie stared at the Queen. 'Loriella?'

Along with Gráinne Mhaol, Mary Read and Ann Bonny, Loriella Desaparecer was one of the most renowned female pirates of the eighteenth century.

'Yes,' Queen Sofia confirmed. 'My father…he has…' Evie waited while the royal gathered herself, sensing an emotional turmoil that was probably rarely seen by anyone. 'It is not openly known yet, but my father has been suffering from early onset dementia for some time now and for the most part we have been managing quite well. He rallied at the birth of our daughter five years ago, but…

there is something about this auction item that he has become fixated on. He has become quite adamant that we obtain it.'

'Why is he so interested in this particular item?' Evie couldn't help but ask.

'My father is convinced that it is the octant that was gifted to Princess Isabella before her travels by the English crown.'

Evie's attention snapped like a band pulled tight. A thousand thoughts and conclusions were weighed, considered and discarded. While one part of her mind delved into what she knew about the eighteenth-century navigational equipment invented only years before Isabella had set sail for Indonesia, another part delved into her own personal history. For years Professor Marin had been working on the theory that Iondorra's eighteenth-century princess had not, as believed, died during the sea journey that would have taken her to her Dutch fiancé in Indonesia, but had in fact become one of the most notorious female pirates of that tumultuous period. And Evie had assisted him. They had scoured research and resources across the world, chasing the tale of the Pirate Princess.

But in doing so they had become the laughing stock of the academic world, made worse when their work was renounced by Iondorra. Evie couldn't blame them for laughing, because it *was* fanciful and *was* the stuff of movies rather than reality. But she had believed in Professor Marin and she had believed where the research had taken them. They just hadn't been able to find concrete proof. But if the Queen was here, taking the sale of the octant so seriously, then perhaps...

'For obvious reasons, we cannot purchase this ourselves. So we would like you to attend the auction in Shanghai, assess the item, and if you feel that it is authentic and identifiable then we want you to obtain it at auction. The Dean of USEL has been apprised that I am in need of your services and has granted you a leave of absence, and we will, of course, pay for any and all expenses incurred.'

Evie's mind was spinning, not with confusion but with what would need to happen if she agreed. The Queen had delivered a summation that was an order she could hardly refuse, but it was one that could cost her greatly. Returning to the research that had made her and Professor Marin a professional laughing stock could be the end of her career.

'I must warn you, even if you are able to find a link between Isabella and Loriella, Iondorra will not be able to acknowledge it. We will soon have to release the news of my father's condition. Talk of Pirate Princesses would be...'

'Devastating,' Evie concluded. 'I understand.' More than most, she supposed, knowing how damaging it had already been to her reputation and her fledgling career. Evie looked around the small lecture hall. For the two years since Professor Marin's death it had been all she had known. No field work, no research. No one wanted to risk their precious funding on a 'girl with no life experience with her head in the clouds rather than the past'. Just stepping outside of the comfort and privacy of her teaching position here at USEL was an enticement. But the Queen was also representative of the palace, who had refused to validate any of Professor Marin's theories, or provide him with access to items and artifacts that would help.

But when Evie looked up at Queen Sofia, beneath the poise and grace she saw a grieving daughter, struggling with losing her father before her very eyes. A daughter who wanted to help her father find peace...find the *truth*.

'Your father, he needs this?'

'I've not seen him so fixated on anything before,' the Queen admitted, the tears of a child for their parent glistening in her eyes.

'"It is not always important that the world knows our history. Sometimes it is enough for just one to know,"' Evie quoted.

'Professor Marin?' Queen Sofia asked with a gentle smile.

Evie nodded, wondering who would be most deeply impacted by this particular truth, if the auction item turned out to in fact have belonged to Isabella.

'I would be happy to go to Shanghai,' Evie decided.

The relief that softened the Queen's tense features was fleeting but enough for Evie to know she had made the right decision. And if the auction item proved to be both from the Pirate Loriella *and* the

Princess Isabella, then perhaps she might even be able to prove that Professor Marin had been right all along. Not immediately—as Queen Sofia had said—but eventually, perhaps. It would have to be enough for her. 'But before I go to Shanghai I will need to go to Spain,' Evie added.

'Spain?'

'It's something I need to help with the octant's authentication,' Evie explained, thinking of Professor Marin's old notebook. And in her mind's eye, she saw a broad, dark figure walking away from her at the graveside.

'Happy birthday!'

Mateo Marin pulled his mobile away from his ear as his mother's squeals of delight pitched into static. He punched the speaker button on the phone and found a space for it on his desk.

Grabbing the presentation for the first meeting of his afternoon, he took a sip of coffee and nearly spat the tepid liquid out. Grimacing as he swallowed, he glared at the phone as he heard his mother ask what he was doing to celebrate.

'Henri is coming over for drinks and a meal.'

'Mateo! Is that all you are doing? How are you ever going to meet anyone if you just sit around drinking whisky with that boy?'

Mateo had no intention of letting his mother know that he met plenty of women—just none that he would spend more than a couple of mutually beneficial and pleasurable evenings with. He had learned that any more and they got ideas that he had no intention of fulfilling.

'Henri isn't a boy any more,' Mateo chided instead.

'You will both always be boys to me, Mateo,' his mother replied. 'But enough. It is time for you to settle down. When are you going to make me happy?'

Mateo stopped, his hand stuck halfway towards the bin with the now crumpled paper coffee cup clenched in a fist.

'Am I not enough to make you happy as I am?' he demanded, the mockery in his tone hiding the bitterness at the heart of his question.

'Of course you are, *mi hijo*.' His mother's soft words barely reached him as his gaze blurred in the middle distance.

She was still talking but all he could hear, all he could see, was her crying in the corner of the kitchen after they had first returned to Spain from England when he was ten years old and utterly helpless to do anything. Over the years he had never stopped trying to make his mother happy, but settling down? No. He slashed a mental hand through the thought. That would never happen.

'Mateo? You *are* still coming over for dinner on Friday?'

'Of course, Mamá,' he replied, finally throwing the cup into the basket, noticing the spray of cold coffee across the paper. 'But I have a meeting I must get to.'

'Mateo, are you at work? On your birthday?'

'Mamá, it's a weekday. Where else would I be?'

'Meeting the woman who is going to give me grandbabies—'

'Bye, Mamá,' he said, hanging up the phone and cutting her off before she could do more damage.

Mateo checked the calendar on his computer, eyeing the back-to-back meetings he had all afternoon with relish rather than distaste. He purposefully made sure that his birthdays were like this. After all, it was just another day in the year, he told himself.

His mobile rang again and he punched the button on the screen without looking at the caller ID.

'Mamá, if you're that serious, I'll go out onto the street, grab the first woman I meet and make as many grandbabies as you need—'

'Well, that's a rather alarming thought,' came the accented male voice that was most definitely *not* Mateo's mother.

'*Cristo*, Henri!'

'What? You answered the phone like that.'

'I didn't see who was calling.'

'That's not on me, *mon ami*. I'm just checking that you're on for this evening. What time do you think you'll be home?'

'Now you really *are* sounding like my mother,' Mateo growled.

'And you're sounding like a child. You're always so moody on your birthday,' Henri practically whined.

As would you be, if for most of your life the day

meant either upsetting your mother or being forgotten by your father.

Mateo bit back the retort and checked his watch. 'You know why, so stop complaining. I'll be back by seven. You, me, a bottle of whisky and a pack of cards. *Perfecto*,' he said before hanging up.

He had five minutes before—

The knock on his door interrupted even the thought of five minutes to himself and before he could even answer, the temporary secretary covering for his utterly faultless, but in this instance flu-ridden assistant, walked in looking half terrified. Mateo bit back a groan. He liked to fill his birthday with as much work as he could to keep himself distracted, but this was getting out of hand, even for a workaholic like him.

'Yes?' Mateo asked of the terrified assistant.

'There is a woman out here, waiting. She's been here some time,' the young man answered, twisting his hands in knots.

'Who is she? And exactly how long has she been waiting?' he asked.

'She said her name is Edwards and she's already been waiting an hour.'

'An hour?' Mateo groaned. He'd wanted to give the young assistant a chance, but clearly he was out of his depth. 'I'm about to go into back-to-back meetings for the rest of the afternoon. She won't re-arrange?' he asked, half hopeful.

'She says she can't, as she has to leave for Shanghai tomorrow.'

Mateo cast a look over his afternoon schedule. 'Tell her that I'll try and fit her in, but I can't guarantee it.'

Any other day of the year he had wiggle room in his schedule for things just like this, but not today.

'Did she say what it was about?' he asked just as the young assistant was leaving.

The temp shook his head. 'Only that it was personal.'

Mateo frowned. He made very sure not to have 'personal' turn up at his office, so he couldn't begin to think what it might relate to. Edwards. The name sounded as if it should be familiar, but he couldn't put his finger on it.

He dismissed the assistant, picked up the file for the Lexicon deal and left his office by the opposite door to the one his assistant used to take him more quickly to the meeting rooms on the floor below.

Evie crossed her legs again and pulled at the form-fitting white shirt she'd thought suitable to make her look professional enough to approach Mateo Marin in his office. But four and a half hours of waiting and she was feeling distinctly *unsuitable*. The seating area she was in was out of direct line of sight of the assistant's desk, but she could hear him typing away, answering phone calls and sighing. A lot.

She'd arrived at the office as early as possible after her flight from London and had come straight to the imposing building that bore Professor Marin's son's name. It should have been familiar, but the sleek, industrial feat of architecture was so far re-moved from the world she'd shared with Mateo's father, it felt unnerving. And she wished for the hundredth time that he'd answered one of her many calls, or replied to the several emails she'd sent in the last twenty-four hours so that she hadn't had to come in person.

She glared at the picture of Mateo looking out of the magazine cover with one eyebrow cocked ar-rogantly, his arms folded across a broad chest that must have had some kind of Photoshop trickery done to it to make it look so imposing. She'd turned to the first page of the article and there he was again, staring directly at the reader—half-arrogant, half-dismissive and all ego—and the first time she'd seen it, the sudden intense heat that had flashed across her cheeks had stung. By the second look the flutter in her stomach had morphed into an angry buzz as she remembered how hurt the professor had been by Mateo's absence from his life. His son's refusal to resume even the most basic communication had dev-astated Professor Marin, who had not once blamed or resented his son's choice.

But it was the third time she scanned the article that made her gasp—because there in a picture cap-tioned as 'The Library', she caught sight of several objects sitting on the wooden bookshelves. A mag-nifying glass, a watch, a wooden box, a compass. They looked as if they had been placed there absent-mindedly. Things that had been chosen to be pre-served, but easily accessible. Things that had made her wonder about their significance, in the same way as she wondered at a copper bracelet at an ancient burial site, or the earthenware jugs recovered from a lost village. Evidence left behind, for years to come. Like the item in the corner of one shelf that pulled on her heart.

The professor's notebook.

The sight of it so familiar that she'd nearly reached out to touch it on the glossy page of the magazine. She heard the assistant sigh and checked her watch. Frowning, she saw it was nearly six pm. Rising uncertainly, she approached the young man's desk, when he looked up at her half in horror.

'You're still here?' squeaked the assistant.

'Of course. I said I'd wait,' Evie replied, unaware why he would think anything different.

'But Mr Marin has left.'

'Left?' Evie asked. 'He left?' she repeated, her voice rising an octave in outrage. 'But I need to see him. It's matter of the utmost urgency.'

'I… I…' the assistant stammered, and Evie couldn't help but feel sorry for a man who was so clearly terrified of his boss. Her anger at being so easily dismissed by the professor's son receded behind the practicality of what she needed to do now that he had left.

There was no way the assistant would share his employer's home address with her, a complete stranger. She had one night to get the notebook before flying to Shanghai and she couldn't waste it.

'Would you…? I'm sorry,' she said, feigning sudden weakness, not even feeling a little bit bad about brushing her palm across her forehead. 'I'll leave, I don't want to be a burden,' she forced sincerity into her words, 'but I feel a little… Could you make me a cup of tea? And then I'll leave?' she offered.

'Of course, of course, I'm so sorry, Ms Edwards,' the assistant rushed out and practically fled from his desk.

Checking the corridor, Evie bit her lip at the act of deception that came worryingly naturally and, heart pounding in her ears, she flicked through the stacks of paper on the desk. She was about to reach for a drawer when she saw a green Post-it note on what looked like a contract with a company called Lexicon.

Courier to M. M, Villa Rubia, Sant Vicenç de Montalt.

Without a second thought she grabbed the note, fisted it in her hand and, grabbing her bag from the sofa where she'd wasted an entire afternoon, she ran to the lift and pressed the button, desperately praying it would arrive before the assistant returned.

When the doors closed and the lift began its descent, she exhaled her relief at not getting caught in a little laugh, and warned herself from getting too addicted to the adrenaline coursing through her veins. She still had to face down Mateo Marin and get him to hand over his father's notebook. But she would do it, because she *had* to.

CHAPTER TWO

MATEO FLICKED AN angry gaze from the road to the display of his ridiculously expensive car. He wasn't ostentatious by nature, but when it came to travel, he liked luxury. He cursed as he palmed the wheel to take the turn that led to his home. He was twenty minutes late. Henri would probably have let himself in already and made himself comfortable, but one thing Mateo detested was making people wait.

It was because of that that he was late himself. He'd got to the underground car park of his office building when he'd remembered the woman waiting for him in the office. By the time he'd got back up to the sixteenth floor, both his assistant and the unknown woman were gone.

Edwards. There was something about that name that rang a dull bell somewhere—

His thoughts screeched to a halt when he saw at least twenty cars on his driveway waiting to drop their passengers off outside *his* front door. Passengers dressed ready for a party. A party that he was apparently hosting but had not yet been invited to.

Henri.

Mateo was going to kill him. Violently. And publicly.

Having parked his car in the garage which, thankfully, was free of guests, he made his way through his house, calling Henri on his mobile. Keeping his head down, Mateo passed uniformed waiters with silver platters of food or champagne, marvelling at his friend's organisational skills, whilst simultaneously worrying at how easy it was to arrange a party at someone else's house without their permission.

'Explain yourself,' he demanded when Henri answered the phone as he nodded a greeting to a couple who recognised him.

Someone stopped him to shake his hand, the face a blur through Mateo's frustration. All he'd wanted was some peace and quiet.

'It was my New Year's resolution to ignore your wishes,' the Frenchman replied with absolutely no shame.

'Excuse me? That was months ago.'

'I know. It's been a great source of pain that you've not noticed me ignoring your wishes all this time, but I'm glad it's now out in the open.'

Mateo came down the hallway and peered into the living area to see Henri, in a tuxedo, surrounded by several people dressed as if this were The Ritz, phone pressed to his ear, grinning back at him.

'I didn't want this,' Mateo said through gritted teeth.

'I appreciate that you hate your birthday, but

I'm bored and wanted a party,' Henri pouted. 'Besides, you work too hard. It's time you let off a little steam.'

Mateo groaned down the phone.

'Go get changed. You look like you've had to work for a living today.'

'Yes, *darling*,' Mateo replied sarcastically to Henri's mock snobbery, spinning on his heel and turning towards the staircase that would take him to his private suite, narrowly avoiding a waitress carrying a silver tray with empty glasses.

'And wear something nice!' Henri called out before Mateo could hang up.

Today had clearly been sent to test him. But at least now the surprises would be done with.

Evie watched the red lights of the taxi disappear into the night before looking back to the sprawling estate before her. Men in full tuxedos and women in sequins and diamonds passed her, barely sparing her a glance as they all eagerly made their way towards the open doors of the brightly lit home.

Evie wasn't exactly unfamiliar with wealth. Carol and Alan had certainly had enough money to have her schooled from home the moment they'd realised her potential. And no one could argue that anyone who owned a townhouse in Mayfair could be anything short of incredibly wealthy. But this? It just…it just didn't fit with Professor Marin. But it *did* seem to fit with the arrogance she had seen of Mateo Marin.

The article had speculated about the life of the wealthy billionaire bachelor. It had covered the charities and foundations that Mateo had sponsored or founded, and barely skimmed the surface of the investment company he'd started with the help of his mother's family connections. The journalist seemed impressed rather than disparaging of Mateo's easy acknowledgement of the help he'd received as a young entrepreneur, and had lauded the fact the billionaire gave back more than he'd been given, not only to his mother's family, but also to other young business-minded people. It seemed that while Mateo traded heavily in the practical, he also dedicated much of his time and focus to clean energy and newly emerging technologies. In short, the journalist—in Evie's opinion—had clearly been swayed by charm and a good PR team, because nothing she'd seen, or heard, had proved a word of that article to be true.

She came to a stop. She'd hoped to speak to him about his father's notebook in private and throw herself on his mercy. But as she took in the party guests she knew that even at her most socially inept she would have realised now was most definitely not the time to approach him.

She was about to leave when someone shouted at her in Spanish.

'What are you doing? Don't just stand there. You're late, so we'll dock your pay, but we still need the help.'

Her knee-jerk reaction was to apologise, to try

to explain in Spanish that he was mistaken. He was dressed in a white shirt and black trousers. Almost identically, Evie realised, to how she was dressed. But…wasn't this an opportunity to at least see if the notebook was still there? And Mateo Marin *had* left her waiting all day. And that *was* after ignoring all her attempts to reach him otherwise. Did a man who had ignored his father for the last three years of his life even *deserve* to have his father's notebook? A familiar heat crept up her spine as she remembered how hurt the professor had been, even as he'd never once spoken badly of his son.

The man was staring at her now as if she was stupid.

Perhaps fate had intervened and given her an opportunity.

'Pues?'

'Sí, señor,' she replied, quickly rushing to follow him as he stalked towards the back of the house.

I'm sorry, Professor, but it's the only way I can see to get what we need.

She quickly gathered that this man was a manager as he directed various waiting staff through the kitchen and around the house, and before he could give Evie a direct order she picked up a tray and decided that the safest option was to collect empty glasses. She exited the kitchen into the hallway just as Mateo came towards her with a phone pressed to his ear.

Her heart thudded once, hard, and then seemed to stop for a second. He was much taller in person, the width of his shoulders—which clearly had *not* been a trickery of Photoshop—taking up nearly the entire breadth of the hallway. He wasn't bulky, but lean. His features, even creased into a scowl, were alluring, the richness of brown in his eyes so deep, she nearly tripped. Her gaze went to the sharp cheekbones and strong jaw he'd inherited from his father. But, unlike the unruly mess the professor had barely bothered with, Mateo kept his beard trim, cut close to the skin—as if he'd made absolutely sure to be as different from the man he'd shared those features with. Everything in him was contained. Neat.

Apart from his hair, which was thick, dark and unruly, as if a lazy hand had flicked a slow curl and it had stuck that way. It matched the way the top two buttons of his shirt were undone, as if he'd just pulled off his tie after coming home from the office.

Once again, her cheeks heated to an almost painful sting, and she pressed a palm to her skin there, for once thankful that her hands were always cold.

'I don't want this,' she heard him say into the phone.

She slowed her steps, worried they might actually collide, as it didn't seem that he'd seen her.

The groan he sent down the phone raised the hair on the back of her neck, and it turned into a shiver that fell down her spine.

'Yes, *darling*,' he growled as he disconnected the call and slipped his phone into his pocket. Evie had to press herself against the wall and nearly lost the tray of glasses as he passed her, barely sparing her a cursory glance.

Oof.

She struggled to right the tray—and her equilibrium—and just about managed it as Mateo Marin disappeared up the large staircase in the middle of the house. Fury pounded in her chest. That was the second time she'd been ignored by Mateo Marin. And the poor woman he'd been speaking to, Evie thought, shaking her head. To have to put up with a man like that! Evie clenched her teeth together. So much for being a bachelor. *Charming*, the magazine had called him. The man was a menace!

Mateo removed his cufflinks and flicked open the buttons of his shirt, tossing it aside onto his bed. There were strangers in his house. There were *waiters* in his house. He rolled his shoulders, trying to ward off the tension headache beginning to form at the back of his neck and temples.

He stared at the half-empty bottle of whisky on the mantelpiece above the fireplace. This was the one safe haven he had. His suite. He had bought the estate for his mother, but she had never lived there, instead claiming to prefer the smaller apartment in the heart of Almería. Rather than sell it on, Mateo had moved in himself, mainly just for this room. His sanctuary.

If the photographer hadn't promised that it would only be the two of them taking the pictures, and not the army the journalist had brought with him to do the interview his CFO had badgered him into last month, Mateo would never have agreed to doing the shoot in here. Thankfully the suite was large enough so that his bed had been out of the picture.

Reaching for the bottle of whisky and the glass beside it, he poured himself a couple of fingers' worth. Maybe he could just hide out here for the rest of the night, he thought, before huffing out a reluctant laugh. Henri would track him down and pull him out by the ear, no matter what he was wearing.

He took a sip of the amber liquid, relishing the explosion of taste and heat of the alcohol on his tongue, and turned to look at the shelves that lined the entire side wall of the room. *His library.* There were several serious work tomes—hardbacks, academic books from his degree—and there were many history books, which would have surprised most of his acquaintances, and were also academic rather than recreational. There were even the adventure stories he'd loved as a child and had somehow not been able to part with all these years.

On those shelves also sat the compass his uncle had given him on his fourth birthday, the magnifying glass his grandfather had given him when he had first returned to Spain with his mother, the wooden box that had held the cufflinks his mother had given him on his sixteenth birthday, and the watch—the first thing he'd bought himself with his first pay cheque. All of those he knew had been captured by the photographer's keen eye. But in the far corner, was an old beaten-up leather-bound notebook that he was barely able to look at, let alone think about.

With a sigh, he threw back the remainder of the whisky and put the glass down on the side. Perhaps it wasn't such a bad idea that Henri had decided to host a party. Mateo flicked the top button of his trousers and stalked into the en suite. Worried about what on earth Henri would get up to next, he decided he didn't have time for a shower before getting back downstairs to check what havoc his best friend had wreaked upon his life.

He ran the taps in the sink and splashed water over his face and neck, and in his haste got water in his eyes.

Cristo!

This just wasn't his day.

He slammed his eyes shut, hoping that the water wouldn't do enough damage for him to need to change his contact lenses, when his phone beeped. Prising open his clear eye, he peered at the screen to see a text message from Henri.

I left your birthday gift in your room. Indulge away, but don't stay up there all night! It's YOUR party after all.

Mateo bit back a groan. Henri was in one of his Shakespearean-level nefarious moods and frankly Mateo could expect anything from a peacock to a Picasso when he opened his bedroom door.

Although it couldn't have been that big, or surely

he would have seen it before he came into the bathroom. Frowning, he pocketed the phone and gingerly opened the door to his bedroom. With one eye still clenched tight to ward off any damage to the contact lens, he peered into the gloom, his gaze finally resting on the outline of a woman's figure.

Bare hands. He would use his bare hands to kill Henri.

Evie had checked all the rooms on the ground floor and there wasn't even sight of a bookcase in any of them. Biting back an internal groan, she'd realised that she would have to follow Mateo upstairs to the second floor. An area that she'd been told was 'strictly off-limits'. Forcing a confidence she didn't feel, she took the stairs one at a time, the gentle sounds of music and easy conversation dying away as she reached the upper floor. Her heart was thumping so loudly and painfully in her chest that the moment she stepped out of sight, she put down the silver tray and rubbed her sternum, taking slow, deep breaths, just as the therapist had taught her.

She'd never once not been thankful to Carol and Alan for making that resource available to her. While they had never been demonstrably affectionate or even comfortable with emotional intimacy, they had done the best they could to meet her practical needs, with nannies who engaged her interest, or tutors to engage her intellect, and a therapist after recognising that being adopted from birth might result in a certain amount of trauma that would need processing.

As she waited for the breathing technique to work, she wondered once again why they had adopted her. They seemed only to want some kind of legacy that befitted them and Evie was never sure that she'd been able to live up to that kind of expectation, no matter how high her IQ.

She brushed the old hurt aside and focused on what she had decided to do. She doubted Mateo would give her the time to explain why she needed the notebook, and with her flight booked for Shanghai tomorrow morning, rather than risk his refusal, Evie had no other option but to simply take it. The idea of something as illegal as theft rankled, but, given that he had ignored his father for the last three years of his life, Evie had a hard time believing he would even notice the notebook's disappearance.

The corridor stretched out to the left and right of her, four doors on each side. She started with the right-hand side of the corridor and pressed her ear against the first door she came to, her hand resting on the doorknob. Mateo Marin had disappeared into *one* of these rooms. But what were the chances he wanted to seek out the library in the middle of a house party? They weren't, after all, in a Victorian romance novel. Her hand paused on the door handle, heart racing, when...

A drunken giggle and a squeal startled her, leaving her with no option other than to pull open the door, throw herself into the room as quickly as possible, and pray that the room was empty.

Eyes clamped shut, half afraid of what she might see, she heard the couple's steps immediately outside the room. Heart in her throat, she spun round and grasped the handle just before someone tried to open it from the other side.

She couldn't be found in here!

'I think it's locked.'

'We're not supposed to be up here, remember?'

'Oh, come on, Marin has so many rooms and we have such little time.'

The door thudded and Evie got the impression of a body backed against the door, followed swiftly by a moan so explicit her cheeks pinked.

'Let's try the next one.'

Thankfully the couple moved off and soon their hushed giggles drifted into a different part of the house, leaving Evie to give a sigh of relief. She turned around, peering through the darkness at the room she found herself in, and gasped. In front of her were rows and rows of bookshelves, all carefully and meticulously ordered, with a compass on one and a wooden box on another. She'd found it!

Pressing her cool hands against cheeks hot from adrenaline, she took in the rest of the room, frowning at the bed she had not expected to see. The magazine had called this a library. Why would anyone…? Her thoughts trailed off the moment she saw the worn leather-bound notebook that had never left Professor Marin's pocket. Along with his glasses, it was what she most remembered about the man who had been more than a mentor to her.

Half convinced she was seeing things, she crossed the room and plucked it from the shelf. She half imagined that the leather was still warm, as if the Professor had only just put it down. Suddenly she was hit with a tidal wave of emotion she simply wasn't prepared for; a sweeping sense of grief, loss and longing for the steady support and belief that only the Professor had ever really given her. Yes, her adoptive parents had met her every material need, but the Professor was the first and last person who had believed in *her,* not in what she could do or what she could provide.

Holding the notebook to her chest, she had half turned to leave when a door behind her opened, and she turned to find, shrouded in light from the ensuite behind him, Mateo Marin staring right at her.

Wearing nothing but a pair of dark trousers, her gaze consumed the sight of him. Her hand reflexively fisted at her side as she took in the breadth of his chest, the dip and curve of the muscles tensing into a v at his waistband, and her breath sighed out of her in a shockingly feminine way.

With one contact lens still a little fuzzy from the water, Mateo ran his gaze up and down the woman in his room standing, somewhat precariously, on a very high, very tantalising pair of heels. He could tell that she was doing the same to him, the heat of her mutual interest reaching out like a tentative touch across his skin and making his breath shake in his chest.

Even for Henri, this was extreme. The almost constant refrain of his closest friend to leave work at the office and indulge in some play time had become boring in the last few years. Mateo had goals he wanted to achieve professionally in order to secure the personal; to make sure that his mother was happy and that those under his care, his friends, his staff, were safe. He had little time for the distraction of women.

'Listen, I'm not sure what you're here for, but I think it's probably best if you just leave,' he said.

The woman simply stared at him blankly and he wished his eye would clear so he could see her properly.

He sighed. 'If you're after money...' God only knew how much money Henri had promised her and once again he cursed his friend. He'd always skated very close to inappropriate, but hadn't once reached it, until now.

'Money?'

He frowned, her accented Spanish a little clunky, and he switched to her obviously native English.

'Yes, money. If that's what you want—'

'I don't want your money,' she said, the stress on the word 'money' almost distasteful in tone.

Cristo, Henri had actually sent him someone who just wanted to bed the bachelor billionaire. He'd been inundated ever since the article had come out.

Some wanted the notoriety, some just the challenge, and this one? He wasn't sure.

'*Querida*, what is it that you *do* want?'

He blinked and his contact lens finally settled to focus on features he'd already become intrigued by. Long dark hair had been gathered into a ponytail, making her appear fresh-faced and innocent in a way that was a refreshing change to the dates he was used to meeting.

Beautiful. She was *beautiful*. In a very classic way. The curve of her cheek drew his gaze and the temptation to reach out and cup it in his palm burned in his chest. Long, thick lashes framed eyes he couldn't quite see and unconsciously he closed the distance between them, wanting to know their colour. She took a half-step back as if surprised by his movement, halting him instantly.

Something about her clothing, the simple white shirt, rang a bell of warning in his mind, but it was barely audible over the blood rushing in his ears. It was enough to distract him from the fact she hadn't answered his question. Her hands were behind her back, pressing her chest forward, and he tried gamely not to stare at the sliver of skin he could see between the buttons of her shirt.

'What's your name?' he asked, surprised by the gravel in his own voice.

'Evelyn.' Whether it was fake or real, the breathless intonation of her name raised hairs on the back of his neck.

He nodded, disconcerted that his body's instinctive reaction to her was threatening to supersede the moral ambiguity of accepting such a 'gift'.

He took a tentative step towards her, and when she didn't back away he took another until he could finally see what he was looking for. Gold, green and mahogany clashed in eyes that to describe as simply as hazel would have been an insult. Swept back from her face, long, dark tendrils of hair cascaded down her back but it seemed that she was as incapable of looking away from him as he was from her.

Something strong and utterly unyielding wove between them and all sense of propriety left his mind. He reached for her then, his hand cupping her cheek, as he had wanted to do, the strangeness of unfamiliarity mixed with a rightness that almost made him dizzy.

What on earth was this woman doing to him?

He saw his own confusion mirrored in her gaze, as if she was as utterly confounded by this as he.

What is this? he wanted to ask, but was also half afraid to. In the back of his mind, something wasn't quite right, but the day, the significance of it, the past few years suddenly pressed so heavily against him that he wanted to throw it all away and lose himself just for one moment.

Evie didn't know what was happening. Only she did. And she *wanted* it. A small part of her mind was banging against an invisible door, trying to remind her of exactly who this was, but she couldn't hear it over the blood rushing in her ears. The scent of his cologne filled her head, a subtle spice and something deeper beneath that, darker and more masculine. Him. She could smell *him*.

Her heart fluttered in her chest and she felt an internal tremble whip through her body. Her body felt heavy and thick as if she was moving through honey. She should tell Mateo to stop. He clearly didn't know who she was or why she was here. But he was looking at her in a way that made her feel *alive*. As if she were taking the first true breath of her entire life. And before she could say anything, he had closed the distance between them and his mouth was on hers and, *oh…*

His lips, soft but determined, were already in motion when they pressed against hers, enticing her mouth to open to him. When his tongue pressed against hers, she was flooded with an intoxicating, brain-fuddling need that started at her toes and raced up to cover her entire body. He tasted like honeyed whisky, heat and hunger. It flashed over her like a fire and only then did she heed the alarm sounding in her mind.

Shaking out of her stupor, she yanked herself back away from him. Her chest heaving as she gulped in desperate breaths. Desire and shock thundered across her over-sensitised skin and a heat she misunderstood morphed into outrage.

Yes, darling.

The words he'd uttered into the phone hit her a little too late, and before she could stop herself she delivered a quick, sharp slap against his cheek.

CHAPTER THREE

THE SLAP SENT a shock through Mateo that he was, frankly, half thankful for. *What was he thinking?* Immediately he stepped back and raised his hands, more to show he wasn't a threat than in surrender.

It had been short and sharp, rather than powerful, and although he felt a gentle burn across his jawline, the woman in front of him appeared to be more surprised by her own actions than he was. Her knee-jerk response seemed shockingly innocent rather than incited by fury.

'Are you okay?' he asked, concerned by the wide eyes staring up at him.

'No, I'm not okay!' she cried. 'Why would you do that when you have a girlfriend?' she demanded, much to his confusion.

'I don't have a girlfriend,' he replied, bemused by the naïve description of his mythical lover. 'Why would you kiss me if you thought I had a lover?' he retaliated.

She frowned, presumably both at his question and his choice of words. 'I didn't kiss you, you kissed me! Do you always go around kissing women you don't know?' she asked as if outraged by the mere thought.

It was on his lips to protest that he didn't, but he just had. He watched as she raised a hand to her mouth and began to suspect that the surprise he'd seen on her features wasn't from the fact that she'd slapped him, but because of the kiss. But surely that much innocence was feigned. He ran a hand through his hair, frustrated with himself as much as the situation. 'Listen, I don't know what you agreed with Henri—'

'Who is Henry?' she asked, nothing but genuine confusion in her gaze.

'Henri,' Mateo said, stressing the correct pronunciation, even as he quickly realised that no one would ever make the mistake of saying his friend's name in such a heavy English accent if they had actually ever met the man.

'You don't know Henri?' he asked, his throat thick with deep discomfort. Had he been so utterly mistaken?

She shook her head.

'I thought you were a gift from my—'

'You thought a *woman* was a gift?' she asked in outrage, as if the arrogance of it alone was a crime.

'Birthday,' he finished lamely, anger at the way she made it sound painted in guilty red slashes on his cheeks. Because he *had* thought she was a gift and he could see now how that *was* bordering on criminal.

Would the ground please swallow him up now?

'What kind of man—?'

'It was a misunderstanding,' he said, taking a step back further away from her as if it could somehow make up for things. 'Please accept my sincere apologies.' He bowed his head, hoping to convey his sincerity, but when he looked up she was frowning at him as if she thought he was worse than the dirt under those rather spectacular high heels, which he could concede, in that moment, he was.

'But if you don't know Henri...' he said, his mind apparently dulled from the illicit kiss that still had its hooks into his brain and body in a rather alarming way, 'then who are you and what are you doing in my bedroom?' he demanded, anger at himself fraying the thin thread of his patience.

'My name is Evelyn and...' She had started out with confidence but faltered on her explanation, by which time he'd finally realised that she was one of the waitresses for the event.

He supposed at least that he should be thankful she *wasn't* here to seduce him. He caught her gaze, it was swimming with so much—anger, heat, but also anxiety—and he stepped back again. He bracketed his temples with one hand and sighed. *Cristo*, what a mess. 'I'm sure that you were told this area is off-limits,' he said with more exasperation than anger.

She stared at him for a moment, looked down at her own clothes, and something flashed in her gaze just before she answered that made him pause.

'Absolutely, sir, I'm sorry. I...needed just a mo-

ment and this was the first room I found. I'll leave.
Very sorry,' she said, backing away from him.

'About the—'

'Not to worry, sir. Happens all the time.'

It happens all the time.

Why had she said that? She could see that it had
confused him too. That kiss…that kiss had fuddled
her mind and dissolved her rational faculties. She
shouldn't have slapped him. He hadn't deserved
that, but she'd been so shocked by…*everything.*
How could she have kissed Mateo Marin? The man
that had ignored her and devastated his father? She
needed to get out of the room, urgently. And without
him seeing that she had the Professor's notebook.

'I'll just be going—' she said, trying to avoid his
gaze and turning in time with the hand she'd concealed so far, holding the notebook. She was halfway
across the room—the *bedroom*…how had she failed
to see that?—when he called out to her.

'Evelyn.' Her name stopped her and she half
turned, reluctant to meet his gaze.

'If you are…having trouble with any of the clients
you cater to, you should let your manager know.'

Evie stared back at him in genuine surprise. 'You
just kissed me. In your…*bedroom*,' she whispered
as if that would make it any less outrageous. 'And
you are advising me to speak to my manager?' She
posed the question slowly in the hope that he would
realise just how ridiculous his suggestion had been.
And finally, he had the decency to look ashamed.

'It was a mistake.'

'Of course it was,' she said, turning back towards the door, confused by the feeling of hurt and disappointment twisting through her chest. She bit her lip to silence herself. Because that kiss had awoken a desire in her that had emerged gasping for air as if it had been suffocated for years, as if each press of his mouth and plunge of his tongue had breathed life into a need she didn't recognise. And now she wanted more and she didn't know what to do with that.

She could accept that he was telling her the truth—that it *had* been a misunderstanding. But couldn't help but feel disappointment that Mateo Marin was a man who had been so willing to simply indulge in such an intimate moment with a woman who had been presented to him as a *gift*.

And then, beneath that, a deeper part she wasn't quite ready to listen to whispered that of course it was a misunderstanding. A man like that would never be interested in a woman like her. That she would only have been kissed if she'd been paid for.

You couldn't even pay me...

She slammed the door shut on those thoughts, too painful to delve into here, where she was still vulnerable after that kiss. Closing her eyes and summoning the strength she had used to get through much more difficult moments than this, she steeled herself and took a step towards the door, when—

'Stop.'

As if he had control over her body, it did as he

commanded. Frozen, she hesitated. Should she run for it? She was so close...

But his hand closed around her wrist and drew her back round.

When had he got so close?

Her breath stalled in her lungs as he peered down at her with an intensity that raised the hairs on her neck. Would he try and kiss her again? she wondered, half hoping he would but half terrified of the thought.

But when she looked up at his face, she saw a mask. A mask that should have concealed the anger thrumming in his body, but didn't. He shook his head and tutted, slowly. 'Now, Evelyn. There I was, thinking that I was in the wrong, and all this time it was you,' he taunted, his voice a honey-covered growl.

'Me?' she asked, heart in her throat as he reached behind her and plucked the notebook from her hidden hand.

'You little thief.'

Mateo clenched his jaws together before he could say whatever else was on his mind. He'd been feeling utterly disgusted with himself when he'd seen what she was trying to conceal in her hand. And this woman—this *thief*—still had the gall to stand there looking at him as if he were *still* in the wrong.

Evelyn. He frowned. The name finally ringing the bell to the end of its peal. Edwards. The woman who had been waiting for him outside his office that afternoon, the same woman who had been his father's assistant.

He huffed out a cynical laugh.

'Nice to finally meet you, Evelyn Edwards.'

She pulled away from his grasp, rubbing at her wrist as if he'd burned her.

'Well, if you hadn't left me waiting for *four* hours I might not have had to resort to *this*,' she said, her hand gesturing around the room as if it explained everything.

'*This* being breaking and entering, theft, and aggravated assault?' he demanded, astounded at the woman's audacity to sound indignant, given the circumstances.

'I did not break a single thing, and as for assault, that was self-defence.'

He rubbed his jaw, her gaze snapping to the place where her palm had connected with it. Yes, he'd definitely deserved that, but he didn't deserve this, he thought, his grip tightening on the notebook she'd tried to steal.

'Was this what you wanted to see me about?' he asked, holding it up. The silly woman could barely contain her desperation. As if connected to the object, her whole body shifted towards it, and he was unaccountably irritated by the motion, his male pride smarting that her only interest in this room was his father's scribbles. It had been all about the notebook from the very beginning. He was such a fool.

'There are many ways you could have gone about this, Evelyn. *This* was not the right one.'

He turned on his heel and walked past her to put the notebook back on the shelf where it had been.

'Wait.' The word punctured the thick, heavy air in the room.

'I…am sorry,' she said, the words ground out between clenched teeth, betraying the fact that she clearly wasn't sorry at all.

He cast a glance back at her, his raised brows showing the truth of his thoughts.

She sighed and tried again. 'I *am* sorry. But it really is a matter of some urgency. You hadn't replied to any of my emails or phone calls—'

'How do you have my number?' he asked, surprised that a woman he barely knew five minutes ago had become a lot more tangled with his life than he could have imagined.

'Your father gave it to me, in case of emergency.'

He felt as if he'd been slapped a second time that evening by her easy, familiar reference to his father. With a follow-up sucker punch that he had been his father's emergency contact, despite the fact that they hadn't spoken in the three years before his passing.

He wasn't sure how to process that information. His relationship with his father had been more than strained at the best of times. It was as if they'd spoken different languages—something about their interaction always rubbed the wrong way, painfully, abrasively and inevitably. Something that seemed to be repeating itself with Evelyn Edwards.

'I didn't come here to stir up old wounds,' she offered apologetically, as if he could even believe that.

'No? Then why is my father's assistant here?' he demanded, just stopping short of adding, *In my bedroom* and *messing with my head.*

'Your father's *assistant*,' she replied with not an inconsiderable amount of bite to her tone, 'is now Professor Edwards.'

Mateo was impressed, piecing together what little he remembered hearing of her. Child genius, high IQ. And yet, she'd clearly been naïve enough to follow his father down the rabbit hole of what amassed to little more than pirate stories and treasure hunts.

'Good for you,' he replied as he looked away in disappointment.

'Do you think you might be able to…?'

He looked up to find a pretty blush on her cheeks again.

'What?'

'Do something about that,' she said, her hand sweeping a circle in the air around his chest, and belatedly he realised he'd held the entire conversation with her whilst shirtless.

Cristo, this woman short-circuited his brain.

'Don't move,' he said, glaring at her for good measure, before he turned and pulled open the door to his walk-in wardrobe, leaving it ajar so that he could hear her if she tried to leave. He grabbed a pale grey shirt from the hanger and thrust his arms into the sleeves with angry, awkward movements. The kiss, his father, the notebook—they all bled together as he pulled at the shirt cuffs and started doing up the buttons slowly enough to buy himself some time to get his head on straight.

Citrus was what she'd tasted like. Sweet citrus and sunrise.

And since when had he become a poet?

Since the first second of that kiss. It had been as if a switch had been flipped and he'd been utterly overwhelmed. It was probably a good thing she'd stopped it when she had because he wasn't completely sure he'd have been able to end it. And she'd been in just as deep as he had, he'd *felt* it, known it as sure as his own name. She was right, it had been utterly wrong of him to kiss her. But the heat and want from her…it had been there beneath the simmering confusion in her gaze, it had been in the little gasp he wasn't sure she even knew she'd made, the opening of her lips beneath his and the tentative tongue—at first—and then…

Whoosh.

They had gone up in flames.

A flicker moved in the mirror in the corner of the room and he clenched his jaw. It didn't matter if they'd burned down Rome, she wasn't here for him. All she'd wanted was his father's notebook. Mateo turned back, finishing doing up the last button on his shirt, came out of the walk-in wardrobe and stalked towards her.

'Better?' he asked, somewhat peevishly.

'Much, thank you,' Evie replied primly and could finally stop averting her gaze so much. Though she wished he wouldn't glare so much. Something about the way he peered at her beneath those strong, dark brows made her feel too similar to how she'd felt when he'd… She cleared her throat. 'As I was trying to explain, I've been hoping to speak to you about your father's notebook.'

'And when you couldn't, you thought you'd just take it instead?'

While she searched for a way to answer that question, her eyes tracked him as he crossed to the mantel above the fireplace and poured a finger of whisky into a crystal-cut glass.

'Want one?' he asked far too casually for her liking.

She shook her head. All she wanted was to take what she'd come here for and get back to her hotel. Being near him after that kiss, it was all too confusing. Her pulse was still racing, and every time he looked at her she felt it almost like a physical touch. She cursed her pale skin as she felt the blush rise again on her cheeks, because without taking his eyes from her once, he lifted the glass, drained it, and poured himself another.

She opened her mouth to advise him to perhaps take it easy, and once again his raised eyebrow dared her to intervene. Pressing her lips together and biting her tongue, she looked around the room, hoping for a reprieve from the intensity of his focus.

She took it all in, even as she felt the hot, heavy

press of his gaze. The bed had surprised her at first, but that was because she had imagined the bookshelves as part of a bigger library. A desk sat between two impossibly large bookcases, in front of a bay window. But the desk itself was oddly familiar; that deep forest-green leather topping the dark mahogany table-top, with drawers either side of the seating area. Perhaps if she got close enough, she'd see a ring mark in the top right-hand—

'It's a different one.'

She glanced back at him, unnerved that he had read her thoughts so easily.

'The desk. It's not his,' Mateo clarified unnecessarily, his tone so balanced she couldn't read the emotion that lay hidden beneath it.

'Mr Marin. This really has been an unfortunate misunderstanding.'

'Of course it has,' he replied, throwing her words back at her.

She ground her back teeth together to prevent herself from saying something stupid. Inhaled, counted to five and exhaled slowly. 'I waited. Outside your office, this afternoon, and when I came here—'

'How did you get my address, by the way?' he interrupted easily, infuriating her—in part because she still felt guilty about it.

'I saw your address on the desk while your assistant was making me a tea,' she said, hoping Mateo wouldn't blame the young, out-of-his-depth staff member.

'Huh,' was all the reply he gave as he watched her

over his whisky glass. 'He's a temp,' he said, half apologetically. 'Of course, had my usual secretary been present, you would have been seen, and sent away again within minutes, I assure you.'

Without the notebook. That was the unspoken conclusion to the sentence she heard. And once again his absolute refusal to listen or try to understand her—just as he had done with his father—grated on nerves already raw.

'I came here to speak to you and explain,' she tried again, 'but there was a party and I was mistaken as a waitress,' she said, gesturing to her clothes and then regretting it as Mateo's slow gaze tracked her body, 'and before I knew it, I had a tray in my hand.'

'Clearly it would have been too much for you to simply explain that you weren't the hired help for this evening?'

She bristled at the superiority in his choice of words.

'Well. Here I am now, listening. Why do you want the notebook so badly?'

'I need it to…to…' Evie bit her lip, remembering the NDA in time to stop herself from breaking it, but clearly managing only to look even more idiotic to Mateo than she had before.

Something flashed in his eyes—as if he'd come to a realisation. 'I can't believe this,' he scoffed. 'You're going after the treasure?' He shook his head at her as if he was disappointed in her. 'It's a fool's errand,' he stated, looking at her as if she had utterly lost her mind. He was shaking his head, even before he said his next words. 'No. You can't have the notebook. I'm doing this for your own good. You'll thank me one day,' he said, pointing a finger at her that she wanted to grab and pull—*hard*.

Anger shot through her, twinning with frustration. How many times had—and would—people tell her what was best for her?

You're not ready for it.

You don't have the life experience for it yet.

It's for your own good.

That heat boiled over into her words. 'Your ego is utterly inconceivable,' she growled at him. 'What on earth would you know about what is good for me? You know *nothing* about me. And yet you think you have the right to decide what is "good" for me?'

He stared at her, all mulish stubbornness, but she thought she had struck a chink in his determination. Until he replied.

'Did he ever tell you of the other historical academics whose careers were wrecked on the shores of this particular pirate story?' Mateo asked. 'Do you know the name Professor Wheller or Kritsen?' It was clear that the names meant nothing to her. 'They were the first two who believed they could prove that Princess Isabella of Iondorra was Loriella Desaparecer. And the reason you've never heard of them? Because they were blacklisted from academia. Men have been driven mad trying to find the Desaparecer treasure.'

'I am not a man,' she replied hotly. 'And I am *not* looking for the treasure.'

'I don't believe you,' Mateo replied. And he didn't. How many times had he heard from his father that it wasn't about the treasure? That it was about history and uncovering the truth, about giving people 'their place' in the story of the past, not the one assigned to them by the victors? And yet still his father had chased the pot of gold at the end of the rainbow as if finding it would somehow make up for the fact he'd lost his wife and son to his madness.

Mateo ground his teeth together. So, no. He knew it was overbearing, and an inconceivable arrogance that Henri would be proud of, but he could not help Evelyn Edwards throw her career and whatever else she had away on a search that she had only pursued because of his father.

'I don't care if you have the backing of the King of England—'

She reared back, shock exploding in her gaze before she tried to blink it away from her eyes. He had strayed too close to the truth. He must have.

'You've *got* to be kidding me?' he groaned, realising that *someone* had to be backing this wild goose chase.

'I don't know what you think is going on but—'

'Enough. I don't want to know and I don't care. Whatever damage you want to do to your reputation from here on in, you do without my help.'

She glared at him. A thousand furies all spitting hell and something in him roared in delight. He felt it, the passion and the heat, boiling the surface of her outrage, until it came to a screeching halt that he felt shockingly jarred by.

She nodded. 'Okay,' Evelyn said, her shoulders slumped, and he had to stop himself from reaching out to her in concern. 'I'm sorry for ruining your birthday. This clearly wasn't what you had in mind,' she said.

Reeling from the sudden about turn, he was so busy trying to find his feet that she spun on her heel and left him alone in his room with the taste of citrus still on his tongue. He reached for the glass of whisky and knocked back the last mouthful, hoping that the burn would erase the last trace of Evelyn Edwards.

Refusing to acknowledge the spool of disappointment that unwound in his chest, he rested his gaze on the bookshelf where he'd placed his father's notebook.

The *empty* space where he'd placed his father's notebook.

That little thief.

CHAPTER FOUR

'YOU ARRIVED SAFELY?'

'Yes, Your Majesty.'

'And the hotel is to your liking?'

'More than, Your Majesty. It's the nicest room I've ever stayed in. I can't thank you enough,' Evie replied sincerely.

Already Queen Sofia had shown more concern over her preferences than her adoptive parents. It wasn't, Are you at the hotel? but, Do you like it? Not, Did you arrive? but, Did you arrive there safely?

'I believe of the two of us,' the Queen said through the phone speaker, 'it is you that needs to be thanked. Did you get what you needed from Spain?'

Did she?

Evie had come to believe that she got a lot more than she'd bargained for.

'Yes, Your Majesty. I got the Professor's notebook.'

'And it will help you ascertain the provenance of the octant?'

'Yes, ma'am. The auction is this evening and I will let you know the moment it's done.'

Ending the call as politely as possible, Evie turned and pushed back the curtain on the incredible suite the Iondorran palace had arranged for her at one of Shanghai's most famous hotels.

The view of the river took her breath away. As the sun crept upwards to meet the day, mist hazing the edges of the serene vista, she knew she was seeing a different image from the typical neon-bright, futuristic marvel that most people associated with the Huangpu. A golden glow pushed at the night's blue slowly, edging it back to make way for the sun. It felt as if she was witnessing a glimmer of the *real* Shanghai.

Evie had wanted to come here for years. She and the Professor had been due to attend the Shanghai Archaeology Conference two years ago but Professor Marin had passed just before. And to be here now, alone, made her feel a little sad.

Seeking comfort, she looked to the notebook she'd left on the bedside table. In the twelve hours of the flight from Spain she'd pored over every page, some of the Professor's notes making her smile, some of them making her cry, and some making her wonder if Mateo had read the words written down by his father.

From his reaction when they had met, she doubted it, sadly.

And just like that, the thought of Mateo did it again—made her heart thud a little heavier in her chest, made her skin a little too sensitive. She pressed her fingers to her lips again, and tried to catch a breath. She bit down gently against her lower lip, hoping to relieve the ache that had taken up place the moment she'd pulled away from his kiss.

And then, just like when she'd tried to get some sleep on the plane, the memories of that kiss morphed into an earlier memory—one that was half-nightmare.

You couldn't even pay me to kiss you.

The one time she'd ever had the temerity to ask someone out and, in her naïvety, had forgotten that she was a sixteen-year-old girl, surrounded by university students in their twenties. Of course, it had ended badly. Shame and embarrassment crawled up her neck in hot, ugly inches. And no matter how she tried to tell herself that what had happened with Mateo was different, the exact opposite even, something had connected them in her mind and she couldn't seem to separate them.

She swallowed the lump in her throat and turned back to the bed. It was six am now and she had five hours before she could see the octant, and then, if it proved to be authentic, she would need to find something suitable to wear for the glamour of the evening's auction. But as she crept between the covers of the bed, yawning, her last thought before falling asleep was of deep brown eyes and hot caresses.

Mateo descended the short flight of steps from the private jet that had brought him from Spain to

Shanghai in a fraction of the time it would have taken Evelyn on a commercial airline, with Henri shouting down the phone in his ear.

'A bottle of whisky! I left a bottle of *whisky* in your room, not a woman! How could you think I'd do such a thing?' Henri demanded.

Mateo pinched the bridge of his nose.

'I mean, I'm a lot of things, Marin, but a procurer of women is *not* one of them.'

'And *that* is the most important part of everything I've told you, is it?' groused Mateo.

'Right. Your Father's pretty assistant—'

Mateo pulled up short. 'I didn't say she was pretty.'

'You kissed her. Is she *not* pretty?'

Mateo clenched his jaw together, cursing that, no matter how much coffee he'd drunk that morning, or whisky he'd drunk last night, he could still taste a sweet citrus on his tongue. 'That is not the point,' he reluctantly replied. 'She stole from me—'

'So you kissed your father's pretty assistant—'

'She's a professor,' he reminded Henri, much in the same way that she'd reminded *him* last night.

'Evelyn Edwards stole your father's notebook and you're in Shanghai to get it back,' Henri replied in loud, sharp words down the phone.

'Yes,' Mateo said, pulling the phone away from his ear and wincing slightly as one of the cabin crew took his suitcase to the black town car waiting for him on the private landing strip. He smiled perfunctorily at the woman who had ideas in her gaze and suggestions on the tip of her tongue, and, ignoring both, he got into the back of the car...alone. 'And while I'm here, I'll be able to meet with Léi Chen.'

'Only you would try to do a business deal while following a woman halfway around the world.'

Mateo pressed against the dull throb at his temples. Contrary to what women—and Evelyn Edwards—seemed to think, he wasn't a notorious playboy willing to bed anyone that entered his bedroom. He still couldn't work out what had come over him last night. He counted his drinks before she had appeared in his room. He'd only had one and that was most definitely not enough to fuddle his mind to the extent that he grabbed and kissed, *thoroughly* kissed, a strange woman in his room, no matter why he'd thought she was there.

'Your message said that you'd left a present in my room.'

'It. Was. Whisky.'

'*Where?* Where did you leave this mythical bottle of whisky?' Mateo demanded for the hundredth time.

'I left it beside your bed.'

'You left it in the darkest corner of my room, not known as the best place for leaving presents!'

'That is beside the point. When you find her, you tell her it's your mistake. I cannot have people out there thinking that I *buy women*.'

'I hardly think that's the most important—'

'You promise me *right now.*'

'Okay, okay,' Mateo said, pulling the phone away

from his ear for long enough to give the driver the name of his hotel, and returned to the call, 'I promise I'll let her know.'

'Listen, don't worry about Lexicon. I know the deal as well as you do,' Henri assured him. Mateo bit back the thread of discomfort at the idea of handing it over to anyone, but he trusted Henri with his life. He'd already caught enough grief when he'd called to cancel dinner with his mother, and leaving work rankled, even if it was just long enough to get back the notebook.

'But are you sure that meeting Léi Chen is the right thing right now? You've not taken a holiday for *years*.'

'This isn't a holiday,' Mateo growled.

'But you're in Shanghai, and with a pretty professor too—'

'I'm hanging up now,' Mateo announced, despite the smile pulling at the curve of his lip. When his entire life had changed in an instant, Henri— the first student he'd met at the exclusive boarding school his mother's family had sent him to—had been the one to make him laugh until his stomach hurt, and smile when he'd thought he'd not find anything to smile about again. Family—Mateo knew— was made of more than just DNA.

It was made from being there when needed. Present and in person. Time and time again throughout his whole life his father had made him wait. Second to a treasure hunt that was scribbled about in the pages of a notebook Mateo couldn't bring himself to read. There had been so many times over the years when his mother had needed her husband. When *they'd* needed him. But instead, it was Mateo who had stepped up to comfort his mother when she cried. He'd been the one who had made sure that his mother had what she'd needed, the security she'd needed. And his father? He'd buried himself in his research, or some dig site that might finally prove his utterly baseless theories about princesses and pirates true.

So yes, he'd come to Shanghai because he wanted that notebook back. If only to burn the thing and be done with it for ever.

In the viewing room of one of Shanghai's most famous auction houses, Evie felt the hushed silence, as reverent as that in any museum. The large warehouse-sized space stored all of the items up for auction over the next forty-eight-hour period, and what she saw was a veritable feast of exquisite historical artefacts, some impressive, some simply beautiful.

Feeling much better than when she had landed, and dressed in clothes that were much more comfortable and familiar to her than the black and white suit she'd chosen to wear to meet Mateo Marin, she made her way slowly towards the area that displayed the items of the auction she was interested in.

Her heels clipped on the concrete floor, polished to a gleam. Her high-waisted, wide-legged trousers concealed the ferocious height of her favourite pair of shoes. It was her only indulgence, she thought, smiling a little at the rather shocking amount of money she'd paid for this particular brand. It wasn't that she was short. In fact, if anything, at five feet six, she was almost tall in some circles. But shoes had become the thing she'd relied on to see her through whatever she faced. She'd been walking through Cambridge, shortly after her first—and last—May ball, her confidence in tatters and her heart low. She'd passed a shop and stopped to stare at the beautiful high heels in the display window.

A girl wearing those wouldn't be laughed at, she'd thought. *A girl wearing those would be confident, alluring. A girl wearing those would be a* woman.

At sixteen years old, not even able to legally drink, having just been humiliated and rejected by her first crush, she'd wanted all those things so desperately. Even now, Evie's breath shuddered in her lungs from the memory of that need. It felt like a lifetime ago, but she remembered the hurt, the pain and the hope. That was the day she'd bought her first pair of heels and she'd worn them for hours and hours, practising to walk in them until she'd mastered it completely.

Yes, she would be embarrassed again, and yes, laughed at too, and she might even have to fake that confidence a little. She might never quite be alluring enough, but she was a woman from that point on in her mind, heart and soul.

And in *this* moment? Utterly sure in her ability and her knowledge of the item she was about to assess, she relished the clip of her shoes echoing in the large space as she drew closer and closer to the very item that could, one day perhaps, give credence to the Professor's final research paper. And maybe, just maybe, help prove her own theories about Princess Isabella too.

There were a few other people in the brightly lit area but she let their hushed whispers disappear into a haze of background noise as she came to the raised glass case containing the gold legs and semi-circles of the eighteenth-century octant up for auction.

A beautiful example of an early edition octant from John Handly (1682-1744), made of gold and ivory. Unique for its unusual design and materials for the period, and the thicker, graduated arc along the bottom. The navigational equipment has exquisite and unusual detailing, with the following engraving:

'Presented by J Berry Aberdeen on behalf of His Majesty King George II. May your travels be swift and take you where you need to go.'

Item reported, without proof, as having belonged to Loriella Desaparecer.

It was a thing of beauty, and not just because of how well it had been preserved. Despite the fact that every inch had been intended to aid navigation, there was elaborate artistry in every curve. And as she came around to the back of the glass box, allowing her to see the back of the octant, she searched for the mark that the Professor had written about in his notebook. It had been a habit of Isabella's father, the King, to place his own mark upon any expensive gifts, in case ownership ever came into question. And there it was! A small but perfectly identifiable etching of the five petals, single stem and leaf of a clematis; the national flower of Iondorra. Just like the one from the old charcoal rubbing Professor Marin had folded into the pages of his notebook.

She peered closer just as she felt someone behind her. When she moved a step to the side to see more clearly, a shadow again fell across her line of sight. Sighing irritably, she turned to confront the person and stumbled the moment she saw who it was.

A strong arm swept out around her waist, holding her, when she would have fallen from heels that had never once let her down before, ever. As she looked up into the eyes of the man who held her, rich dark whispers of heat were interrupted by a cynical glare.

'Fancy meeting you here,' Mateo Marin said with absolutely no surprise whatsoever.

Her hands clutched at his waistcoat and the *heat*… He felt burned, deeper than his skin, so much so that he nearly dropped her.

Mateo cursed. He could read volumes in the gaze staring up at him, marvelling at the clarity of each emotion he saw. And while his mind chose to ignore the flash of desire he sensed she struggled with, his body didn't. Fighting back his own arousal, he righted her and looked away from the pink flush across her cheekbones. He pulled once sharply at the points of his waistcoat, needing something to do with his hands other than reach for her again.

'What are you doing here?' she demanded with a bite no more dangerous than a papercut. She glared at him angrily from beneath long lashes he remembered being fascinated by. 'Wait, how did you...how did you find me?' she demanded, passing a leather briefcase from one hand to another.

He shrugged as if he hadn't paid an inconceivable amount of money to hire someone to find precisely that information out. 'It wasn't that hard.'

'You had me investigated?' she cried in realisation. 'That is a violation of my privacy!' Her outrage would have been laughable, had it not been for the increasingly concerned glances being cast their way from the other people in the warehouse.

'You can't have expectations of privacy while committing a crime.'

'Oh, for the love of—'

'Give me back what you stole and I'll be out of your life for good,' he said pleasantly, even though he felt anything but pleasant.

Her hand flexed around the strap of her bag as if she thought he might try and take it from her with force. *Joder*, what kind of man did she think he was? And then he remembered that she had been grabbed and kissed by a stranger in a dark bedroom and told that she had been mistaken for a gift.

'And to...erm...' Mateo rolled his eyes to the ceiling. 'Henri wishes for it to be known that he doesn't buy women.'

'What?' Evelyn's hazel eyes peered up at him in confusion.

Mateo cleared his throat. 'I promised that I would explain to you that Henri did not buy a woman for me as a gift.'

'Oh.' She bit her bottom lip and snared his attention away from the conversation. 'Okay,' she said on a little laugh. This was *not* going how he'd intended. People didn't laugh at him; they usually did what he said. But Evelyn Edwards seemed to oppose him at every turn.

'Now, the notebook?' he asked, holding his hand out in expectation.

'I can't give it back to you,' she said.

'I believe you can. It's really quite simple. You reach into your bag and you place it in my hand.'

'I don't have it with me,' she replied, the pretty blush becoming slightly angry on her cheeks now.

He raised an eyebrow, disbelieving her entirely.

'And even if I did,' she started, 'why do you want it?' she asked, for once genuinely. 'What is it to you? You didn't speak to him for the last three years of his life, Mateo.'

And there it was again. The knife that cut too close to the heart of an old hurt it left him almost breathless with anger.

'You think you have more right to it than I do?' he demanded.

'Maybe, yes,' she replied, and the sheer honesty of her response was more cutting than a thousand knives.

'Well, you're wrong,' Mateo stated sharply. 'I deserve every page of that notebook because while he was scribbling notes about his research on his trip to the research dig in Indonesia, he'd promised to be there for the results of my *bachillerato*. And when he was delivering his lecture on Iondorra's Economic Impact on Europe in the Eighteenth Century, it was my twenty-first birthday. And you know what? I don't even know where he was to celebrate my company's IPO launch because all I *need* to know is that he simply couldn't be bothered to show up.'

Evelyn looked at him with a sympathy that grated rather than soothed.

'Have you read it?' she asked.

'I don't need to read it. And neither do you. You were there with him on every dig and every research paper,' he bit out, unable to prevent the mean words from spilling between them.

'I don't—I'm sorry, Mateo.'

'But you won't give the notebook back to me?'

Evelyn bit her lip as if to stop herself from saying more.

'Fine. You don't want to give me the notebook? Then I'll have to take something you want even more.'

Concern filled her gaze, blotting out the thousands of questions he saw there. Honestly, her eyes were like a constellation, mapping the course of her thoughts. The woman should never play poker. Because he'd already beaten her at her own game.

'A word of warning. If you're planning to go to the auction dressed like that, think again.'

With that parting shot, he turned on his heel and stalked out of the auction house, leaving her standing alone in the middle of a near empty room.

Evie flexed her hand, before running the black liner across her eyelid, working carefully so as not to stab herself. Much like the heels, she'd practised make-up but it had never made her feel the way that the shoes did, so she tended not to wear it. She always thought that when teaching, it made her look as if she were trying too hard. To fit in, to look older, to try to make them take her seriously. She pulled her hand back as she got a little upset.

Why was she thinking like this all of a sudden?

Because she was still upset about Mateo. Only upset didn't seem to cover the seething mass of emotions that twisted and turned whenever she thought about that afternoon. She felt guilty, because at the beginning of their encounter she truly hadn't wanted to give the notebook back to him. She *hadn't* believed that he'd deserved it more than her and facing that thought was difficult and painful.

Mateo's words had conjured a side of the Professor unknown to her and it seemed he was not entirely blameless in the one-sided relationship she'd seen and that was also difficult. But Mateo had also been wrong about his father not being bothered to be there for him, and once she had returned the octant to the Iondorran palace, she would make sure that Mateo not only had the notebook, but also understood that the Professor had bitterly regretted some of his choices.

And between anger and guilt, she was annoyed with herself for the utter extravagance of the dress she had eventually bought. She'd let Mateo's taunt get to her and, even though she hadn't quite understood what he'd meant by it, it had sunk teeth into her vanity and hurt.

She turned side-on in the mirror, casting a critical eye over what she saw. Red sequins covered every inch of the material that clung to her skin like water, flashing and sparkling in the bright bathroom lights. The deep v on her chest was replicated on her back, and the ruby-rich red colour of the material made her skin glow. The skirt flared out from the knee and pooled in a half-train behind her.

A secret feminine part of her was both giddy and thrilled, she really did look good, but the other more practical part chided the waste of it. Would Mateo even see her in it? The warning he'd left her with… did that mean he intended to come to the auction? Evie was confused by her feelings. That she wanted him to see her like this, that she wanted him to… *want* her.

Not that it mattered. It wasn't as if she would ever act on it. Mateo had already proved how utterly unsuitable he was. Someone like him would never understand someone like her. She rolled her shoulders and pulled herself together. Tonight, she would bid on the octant, tomorrow she would travel to Iondorra, and the following day return to her flat in London, where her normal life would resume.

Barely an hour later and Evie found a seat near the large, heavy-curtained window as the seats at the auction quickly filled up. Tuxedos, velvet, silks, and jewels were as on display as the items up for sale. While the evening auctions often held fewer lots than those in the daytime, the money changing hands that night would likely exceed sixty million, and people dressed for the occasion. People that, she was sure, would bid on the octant.

She sat through the early lots trying not to think of where Mateo was. Casting her eyes almost constantly around her, she'd not yet seen him. Maybe he wouldn't show up after all?

'Lot Thirty-Two, ladies and gentlemen, an unusual octant thought to have belonged to the great pirate Loriella Desaparecer.'

A gentle ripple of laughter broke out, cresting against her like a wave, and Evie fought back the irritation and frustration it caused in her.

'While octants of the period usually sell for much less, this unique piece made with gold accents not only increases interest, but so does the inscription, connecting the item to the British royal family. Owing to significant interest, we'll start the bidding at five hundred thousand.'

There was a gasp across the audience. Even Evie

hadn't expected the guide price to be so high. It differed from what was in the catalogue. A gentleman near the front started with the first bid, she countered, and so it began. The three or four other interested parties soon dropped away as the bidding got closer and closer to one million. Her heart was pounding and a cold sweat was breaking out across her skin as they got closer and closer to the Queen's financial ceiling. Evie had a certain amount to play with, but any more would bring too much attention to the item and Iondorra still couldn't risk anyone discovering their interest.

Back and forth she went against the man in the front, who didn't seem bothered in the slightest. Unease filled her as they were now at the nine hundred thousand mark. So much for avoiding attention. The other bidders were now watching a tennis match as she and the man bid back and forth. She wanted to scream. Gripping the white card with her bidding number on it, she raised it to bid nine hundred and ninety thousand.

Her heart beat painfully in her chest as she saw the man waver. It was going to be hers. She would win the bid on the auction and be able to return to Iondorra with it. The Queen would be able to give her father the peace he deserved and she might be able to use it to find proof that would finally validate the Professor's research. Wet heat pressed against the back of her eyes and she willed herself not to cry with hope.

'The bid is with the lady in the middle. Back to you, sir?'

She bit down on her lip. She couldn't afford to bid any more if he chose to counter.

The man shook his head.

'Going once…'

She stifled the sob of hope and excitement that filled her chest. She was going to do this. She was going to get the octant.

'Going twice…'

'Two million dollars.'

In unison with every other person in the bidding gallery, Evie turned to look at the man who had just doubled her bid and the gasps of shock were drowned out by the sound of blood rushing in her ears.

There, at the top of the aisle at the back of the room, dressed in a black tux, sexy as sin with his hair in effortless disarray, was Mateo Marin, who had just bought the octant for two million dollars.

CHAPTER FIVE

MATEO MARIN FIXED his stare on the auctioneer, because if he caught even the merest glimpse of Evelyn Edwards he might just implode. He should have spent the last six hours since he'd seen her working on the prep for his meeting tomorrow with Léi Chen. The merger would be a real coup if they could pull it off, bringing untold solidity to his financial base. That security…it was important to him. But instead, he'd been distracted by thoughts of Professor Edwards, so much so that he'd sent at least five emails to the wrong recipient and had nearly caused an internal incident. Henri had finally got on the line and told him to switch off his laptop, making him feel even more frustrated. And now? The victory he thought he'd feel at snatching away the precious item she'd clearly come to buy from her at the last second…it hadn't helped one bit.

Evelyn turned to glare at him, ignoring the gossips in the seats beside her flicking their gazes between the two of them. Eyes rimmed with kohl made the deep chestnut of her irises glow golden. Her lips were a shade more intense, not powerfully rouged, but accented in a way that made her look freshly kissed. The subtle make-up stirred far too much of a reaction in him and he made to turn away, and then she stood up.

Cristo.

Tension hummed through his body as if he'd been shocked by mains electricity and he was forced to almost violent levels of self-control to stop himself from doing something monumentally stupid like reaching for her the way he had in Spain.

A red shimmering film clung to a body he'd not even had the faintest idea about. Hidden beneath the trousers and shirts he'd seen her wear was a body that rooted him to the spot. He failed terribly to stop himself from consuming her with his gaze, lingering over the span of a waist he wanted to encase with his hands, the shoulder he wanted to slide the silken strap of her dress from, the breasts he wanted to take into his mouth and hear her cry her pleasure. And then, when she started to walk towards him, the sheer sensuality of the glide of her hips on those incredible heels, and he had to turn away or embarrass them both. It had been too long since he'd allowed himself to be distracted by a woman and he had no intention of starting now.

At the back of the room an assistant was waiting to direct him to the clerk to process the paperwork for the sale, but he too was as lost to Evelyn as Mateo had been. The young kid's blush put Mateo firmly back in his place and by the time Evie had reached him, Mateo had regained control over his wayward body.

'What was that?' she demanded in a furious hiss.

'That was me showing an interest in eighteenth-century pirate treasure.'

'Don't be absurd,' Evelyn dismissed. 'You have never once shown an interest in—'

'Cara,' he said, interrupting her, 'please know that when I show an interest in something my focus is absolutely, utterly and irrevocably fixed.'

She glared at him, and golden fury rained down on him like the bright embers of a children's sparkler. Everywhere her gaze touched him burned bright but left no damage other than to his libido.

'You are holding it hostage,' she growled, and he was half surprised that she hadn't stamped her foot.

'The octant? Yes. I am,' he replied and had to work to stop himself from smiling at her indignant outrage.

He took her arm, ignoring the sparks the physical contact sent up his skin to his chest and, turning them away from the curious glances, led her out of the auction room into the reception area.

'I would have given you the notebook back,' she said from between clenched teeth.

'Would have?'

'Well, I'm not going to now, am I?'

'It's sweet that you think you can stand toe to toe with me on this. You *will* give it back to me,' he warned, before turning to find the office where the clerk waited to process the paperwork.

* * *

Evie paced the reception room, waiting for Mateo to return. She told herself off for letting him get to her. It was the octant she needed, not the notebook. Of course, she should give it back to him, as she'd intended from the beginning. But Mateo's high-handedness had riled her usual peaceful and happy equilibrium. And to think…she'd been actually hoping that he'd show up to the auction and see her in the dress!

And now everything that the Queen had wanted was at risk. Yes, Evie had hoped that she might be able to prove her and the Professor's theories true, but more than that she had really wanted to give a daughter the chance to do something kind for her father.

Just then the devil walked back into the room and she hated that even through the angry red mist she could see how gorgeous he was. His hair was tousled as if he'd been running his hands through it, his eyes looked darker against the midnight colour of his tuxedo. At some point Mateo must have pulled his tie loose, as the ends hung down, stark against the white cotton shirt, making him look every inch the billionaire Lothario.

She bit her lip and dragged her gaze upwards, to discover that he had caught her staring. He raised his eyebrow as if to dare her to keep looking, but she couldn't and turned away.

'Are you coming?' he asked her.

'Where to?' she asked hesitantly.

'Somewhere we can talk privately.'

Gone was the surface civility from before, the good-natured, easy-going façade he had hidden behind. The tone of his voice and the taut lines holding his body stiff all spoke of the fact that the games were over. Even the slight undercurrent of flirtation that had simmered between them ever since the kiss was gone.

She nodded and followed him from the auction house. They didn't speak a word to each other in the taxi that took them back to the hotel they were both staying in. She didn't object as he led them through the exquisite foyer of the hotel, towards a bank of lifts that looked very different from the ones she used to get to her room.

She didn't say a word as he gestured for her to enter the lift and swiped a card that permitted access to the penthouse. She barely registered that the doors opened directly into the suite that looked out over the river and the stunning nightscape of Shanghai as she tried to find a way through thoughts that circled between the octant, the Professor, Princess Isabella and Mateo and his father. And lost amongst all of them, buried deep in there, were thoughts about herself.

She placed her wrap over the arm of the sofa and turned to where Mateo watched her from the entrance of his suite. The wooden box containing the octant was tucked under his arm, possessively.

'Can I see it?' she asked tentatively.

He seemed to consider her request and for a moment she thought he might refuse it, but he slid the box onto the coffee table in front of the sofa.

'Knock yourself out,' he said before going to the wet bar and pouring himself a drink.

Evie rounded the sofa and, sitting, took a breath as she opened the box.

'How much do you know about your father's research?' she asked as she took in the exquisite craftmanship of the octant up close. It really was a thing of beauty.

'Assume I know ninety per cent and understand eighty per cent.'

She smiled sadly at his response. 'Your father used to say the same thing.'

'I remember.' The sharp edge of his tone lashed and stung.

Forcing down the feeling, she delved into the legend that had captured her attention at a very young age and been the driving force behind her desire to delve into archaeology in the first place.

'Princess Isabella had been sent by her father, the King, to her fiancé in the Dutch East Indies—a Dutch colony in what is now known as Indonesia—when her ship was attacked by pirates.'

'There was a great battle,' Mateo said, picking up the train of the story in an overly dramatic fashion. 'The Princess's people put up a valiant fight, enough so that the pirate captain was killed in the skirmish,' he concluded, and then he frowned as if, for the first time, realising the story had a plot hole. 'Everyone thinks Isabella also died during the attack, but my father believed she survived. So why didn't she make it to her fiancé?'

'Rumour was that he was a particularly vile man with a reputation for cruelty who only wanted the dowry, not the wife. And he'd already received the dowry.'

'He intentionally let his fiancée get set upon by pirates? If she survived, why didn't she just go home?'

Evie let out a half-laugh. 'She was betrothed to a Dutch duke in a trade exchange. She was nothing more than a chattel and her father would simply have sent her back to Indonesia to her fiancé. There's reason to believe that she was ignorant to that.' Unwanted by parent and fiancé. Even as a child she had unconsciously identified with a princess disowned by her family and her future.

'And she just walked into the position of captain? A princess?' Mateo asked sceptically.

'I doubt it was that easy. But within eighteen months, Loriella Desaparecer was sailing the high seas and causing more damage to the Dutch East India company than any other pirate or privateer operating during that time. The records are sparse and much of what we know is hearsay. But that's not surprising, as the records are from the VOC— the Dutch East India company. And it's unlikely that her ex-fiancé would want any specific details getting out about the beating they were taking from his betrothed.'

'You believe it,' Mateo observed, 'that they were the same person.'

'Yes, I do,' she answered honestly, squaring up to him as if she expected him to meet her with a barrage of doubt and derision.

'And you think this octant is proof of that?' he asked.

'No,' she replied, immediately confusing him a little. 'It is clearly possible that Loriella stole it from whoever ransacked Isabella's boat, or was given it, or it fell into the sea and was discovered later. There are many, many ways in which the octant that once belonged to Isabella ended up with Loriella.'

'Then why do you want the octant?'

'I don't, but someone else does, very much. And I will do anything I can to make that happen,' she said.

'Even give me back my father's notebook?' he asked.

She was torn. He could see that. Her connection to his father was almost visceral and tied to that damn notebook.

'You paid two million dollars for the octant,' she stated quietly.

'A price I am willing to pay to put an end to this once and for all,' he replied before finishing his glass of whisky in one mouthful.

'But don't you want to know?' she asked, her large eyes glowing with an earnestness he felt too old for.

'Know what?' he asked, suspecting he didn't want to hear the answer.

'Know if he was right? Know if this could help even with the smallest possibility, prove that your father's theories about Isabella were true?' The plea in her voice, the eagerness, the desperation to redeem his father…it was as painful as it was obvious.

'No. The veracity of his claims about Isabella in no way makes up for all the time he spent ignoring his duties as a husband and as a father. He just wasn't there, Evelyn. He was *never* there. Again and again he was absent from my life and you don't know what that's like, how it makes you feel.'

He could have bitten off his own tongue. Even if he hadn't just remembered that she had been adopted and taken in by an rich, older English couple, the look on her face—the way that the blood had drained instantly from her features, the sheer excavated wound that her eyes exposed—was enough. He remembered his father's complaints from back when they were still talking; frustration and incredulity at the behaviour, the *absence*, of his assistant's parents. He'd called them cold, aloof, and utterly unfeeling. Mateo had remembered because he'd not been able to understand how his father couldn't see the irony of what he was saying. That his father was raging against the injustice of bad parenting had been a knife in his gut. And even now he remembered the twisting feeling of it but still that gave him no right to trample all over her pain.

'Evelyn—'

She held up her hand, bringing his silence while she gathered herself.

Guilt scratched against his skin like sandpaper and he couldn't stay still. He put his glass on the side and came to the chair angled ninety degrees from where she sat on the sofa. He sat and braced his arms against his thighs.

But before he could speak, she stood, rubbing her hands on the silk of her dress.

'You want the notebook in exchange for the octant? You're willing to do that?'

'Evelyn—'

'Are you?' She looked up at him as if she wanted this over and quickly.

'Yes,' he replied, the word ground out between clenched teeth, ignoring the swipes his conscience was taking at him.

'Here,' she said, reaching into the briefcase she had brought with her to retrieve the notebook she'd taken from his estate in Spain. 'I never should have taken it. And if I had any other option, I would not be bartering the octant for it now. But before I go, I want you to see something,' she said, unwinding the leather string keeping the cover bound and preventing several loose pages tucked neatly into the spine from coming free. She turned to a page bookmarked by an old Polaroid.

Just the sight of the black square backing the old photograph brought a deluge of memories of the way his father had eschewed the modern technology of digital cameras over the old-fashioned physicality of his Polaroid camera. His mother still had several pictures his father had taken from when he was younger and when they were still together.

'I know that things had become strained between you. And I know—more than most—how lost your father could get in his work. His focus and drive was something that very few people could match, but it came at a cost. One he regretted bitterly.'

Her words should have soothed—wasn't it what he'd always wanted? For his father to have known how much he'd missed out on? For his father to have recognised the damage he'd caused? But they were too little, too late, and he wanted her to stop. Stop explaining and justifying his father's absence.

She plucked the Polaroid from the notebook.

'We were coming back from a conference in Toronto and he'd made sure that our flights stopped in New York. He'd been so excited. So proud.'

Mateo's jaw was clenched so tight, a headache had begun to form. He didn't want to know what she was alluding to, didn't want to hear it. He'd become a child again, pressing his hands over his ears so as not to hear his mother's heart-wrenching sobs.

'We arrived just as you were being interviewed,' she offered as she held out a photograph he couldn't bring himself to look at yet. 'You'd just taken your company public in a record-breaking launch. And they were asking who you had there with you to celebrate.'

'And I said I had everyone I needed,' Mateo replied, remembering how angry he'd been that his father hadn't been there. 'My mother, my grandfather and my friends,' he said, repeating the words he'd said to the journalists that night. It had been the final straw. That his father hadn't been there for his greatest achievement had drawn an uncrossable line between them. But now Evelyn was saying that he *had* been there?

'We left shortly after. He didn't want to spoil your day.'

Finally, Mateo looked at the Polaroid she held out to him.

In the picture his father was standing in the foyer of the New York hotel Mateo had hired for the launch party celebration. His father was staring straight at the camera, beaming with a pride Mateo barely recognised. Mateo's heart pounded as he searched the image for the incontrovertible proof of what his heart wasn't ready to accept. And there in the background, over his father's shoulder, looking up and staring towards the camera he saw *himself*. Goosebumps broke out on his skin as he stared at the little Polaroid. A moment in time he'd never known about.

His breath left his lungs in a gush as if he'd been punched in the chest. 'I…' He didn't even know what to say.

'I know that this doesn't make up for things, Mateo, but you should know that he did love you,' Evie said, hoping that he believed her. 'He did regret the distance between you.'

'Why didn't he just stop? Stop this ridiculous

search,' he asked of the only person who might be able to answer.

'I think...' She hesitated and his heart held its beat. 'I think it's because he wanted to prove to you that it was worth it. That his sacrifice had been for something real.'

'Then why didn't he say anything?' he demanded, his voice like gravel.

'He didn't think he deserved your forgiveness,' she said quietly.

Mateo cleared the thickness from his throat with a cough and reached for the whisky to swallow all the other emotions clamouring to escape. He couldn't stop himself from wondering if things had been different, if he'd seen his father there before giving that interview, would there have been peace before his father had died? Would they have reconnected?

He felt the weight of Evelyn's gaze on him, almost as palpable as the dawning realisation that he had got things so very wrong.

'Who was he to you?' Mateo asked, looking to Evelyn, now standing by the window, having given him some space to process his emotions.

The question might have appeared strange but Evie didn't mistake it for anything other than a child trying to understand their parent.

'He was a lot,' she admitted truthfully.

'How did you meet?'

Evie huffed out a gentle laugh. 'Carol and Alan, my adoptive parents, took me to meet him when they realised my interest in Iondorran history wasn't just a phase. We'd taken a summer holiday to Iondorra when I was about five. They'd already started to notice that my intellect was high. I was apparently dissatisfied with explanations that would pacify other children; my reading skills were beyond above average. At first it was thought that I was an only child used to adult company—Carol and Alan were hardly ones for baby talk or play. But they'd been advised to take me away on holiday and it happened to be to Iondorra.'

Evie turned away to the stunning nightscape reflected in the river just beyond the hotel. 'They had picked up a travel book, hoping to perhaps keep me from asking them questions every two minutes, and I'd read it front to back in less than an hour. There was a small history of the monarchy in it and something about Isabella caught my imagination. I wanted to know more. I needed to know what happened to the woman who had been sent away from her home and never reached her destination.

'We visited the museum and there was a section with Isabella's room recreated with some horribly frightening waxwork figures and pieces of her clothing and jewellery that had remained behind to be sent on once she'd arrived in the Dutch East Indies. And that was it. I was fascinated by the idea that there were belongings, proof, evidence of a life even after it had been left behind.' Evie ran out of steam and realised that she'd just let that all blurt out and her cheeks flamed, and she was suddenly embarrassed. Pressing her cool hands to her skin, she smiled ruefully.

'So it was Isabella that led me to your father. And it was your father that seemed to be the first person I'd met that understood me,' she finished with an apologetic shrug, hoping her words didn't reignite Mateo's hurt.

When she looked up, she was surprised to find that Mateo had left the chair and crossed the room. He was further away than he had been in Spain, but her heart still fluttered in her chest like a bird. The scent that had almost hypnotised her before was still there, taunting her. Hope for something she did not want to name still filled her lungs, making it hard for her to catch a breath.

He looked at her, his gaze unfathomable, but long and steady, as if telling her that he saw her too. Not that he understood her, but that he *saw* her, and that was almost too much for her to bear.

She went to turn away, but his hand caught her chin and gently guided her back. 'Don't. I... I'm glad you had that with him. I'm glad he was there for you in a way that you needed.'

She wished he wouldn't use words like *need* when he was that close to her, when she was this vulnerable. He was talking about his father, and all she could think of was how he'd kissed her. How he'd prised open her lips with his own, how his tongue had filled her in a way that made her both full and hungry at the same time.

Her breath caught and he dropped his gaze to her

lips. Desire flashed like fireworks in the espresso-rich depths of his irises. For an exquisite moment he leaned towards her, the move barely perceptible, but enough for her to feel the puff of his breath against her lips. She angled her head towards him just when he released her from his touch and stepped back as if to emphasise the distance he wanted between them.

Desire turned to shame in a single twist of a heartbeat. Once again she was that naïve girl with her first crush, humiliated by how badly she had misread the situation.

A sob replaced hope, hurt replaced desire and she quickly spun away from him, half running to get her wrap and the box containing the octant. She had to get out of there before she made an even bigger fool of herself.

'Evelyn, wait,' he called after her, but it was too late. Tears were already blurring her vision, but as she blindly reached out for the wooden box it slipped in her cold hands and crashed to the floor, hitting the side of the table, cracking open and landing on the octant.

The gasp that cut through the room echoed with Mateo's own shock as he pulled her back just in time from reaching for a jagged metal piece and cutting herself. Cursing, he led her over to the couch, leaving her only long enough to pour a measure of whisky into a glass and making her drink it. His own shock was almost as acute as hers.

'It's okay, Evie,' he said, using the shorter version of her name for the first time and not even noticing.

'Oh, my God.' She looked up at him, eyes wide and tears gathering. 'I'm sorry, I don't... I'm sorry.'

He shushed her gently and took the octant carefully from her to inspect the damage. Casting his eye over it, he could tell that the bottom arc of the device was a little bent, but it was the crack in the bone inlay along the back of the arc that was the most obvious. His heart dropped, even as he tried to comfort her.

'This can be repaired,' he lied.

But she shook her head back and forth. 'It doesn't matter. It's not about whether it can be fixed...' She held her hand out for it and he gave it back to her, watching as she gently ran her finger over the crack. She shook her head again, but then stopped. Frowning, she brought it closer to her face as if she'd seen something.

'What is it?'

'I don't know... I think... Is that paper?' she asked, seemingly of herself. 'Can you pass me my bag?'

He retrieved the leather briefcase she'd dropped by the door of the suite and gave it to her, taking a seat in the chair beside the sofa.

After rummaging around in the bag, she took out a pair of tweezers and gently went at the crack in the octant, poking the tweezers into the crack and retrieving what looked like the smallest roll of paper he'd ever seen.

He stared in disbelief as she put the octant to

one side, and gently prised open the ancient piece of paper.

'What are they?' he asked, even though he had a sneaking suspicion that he knew very well what the figures were.

Evie looked up at him, shock turning to surprise, excitement replacing horror. 'I think... I think they might be coordinates.'

CHAPTER SIX

MATEO WISHED SHE wouldn't pace like that in the suite. With every movement she made, sequins shimmered and shivered across her lithe form and he couldn't look away. He ran a frustrated hand through his hair and bit back a curse, turning to glare at the tiny piece of paper with numbers scratched onto it from four centuries ago as if it were to blame.

'I understand,' Evelyn said into the phone she'd been on for the last half-hour. 'Yes, I agree.'

Angry. He was angry. A worryingly large amount of pent-up energy was coursing through his veins and he realised that he'd subconsciously been echoing Evelyn's movements and pacing the suite himself.

Basta ya.

He caught her eye and gestured to the door to the bedroom and en suite. She nodded absently and went back to her phone call. He stalked through the door, past the large bed that taunted him, and into the bathroom.

Running the cold tap, he splashed water on his

face in an attempt to shock him out of whatever funk he was in. But in his heart of hearts, he knew it wouldn't work. Because what he felt in that moment was guilt. Guilt, anger, frustration. Had his father been right? All these years, all the anger and hatred he'd directed towards him for choosing to chase a fantasy over his responsibilities, and in actual fact his father had been the only one to see the truth?

He punched the marble countertop in a fit of fury. He wanted to roar, to yell, to swear and break, but Evelyn was only a room away and he didn't want her to see that. Evelyn, the woman who had been the only one to support his father.

It didn't make up for the fact that his father had never been there for him—even if he had been there at the IPO launch. It didn't make up for the fact that his mother had been devastated by his absence, it didn't make up for the years of feeling second best to a myth, a legend only his father believed in. But... if it was real, if those co-ordinates, or whatever lay at the end of them, proved that his father had been right, that *Evelyn* had been right, then maybe he could at least see his father's search through to the end. It was all that was left of their relationship and he owed it to them both to see it through. He could work with Evie, they could take some time to make a plan. He could still see Léi Chen tomorrow and then—he nearly laughed at himself—they could go on a treasure hunt?

Mateo had looked up the coordinates on his phone while Evelyn had called the person she had

been acting on behalf of. Mateo was half-sure it was
the Iondorran palace, but he doubted she'd tell him
even if she was allowed to. The coordinates had pin-
pointed an island in Indonesia and he knew that she
would want to go there.

Cristo, he wanted to go there. It became an urgent refrain in his mind, needing to know if his father really had been right. Maybe knowing one way
or another would finally bring him and his mother
some peace.

He stared at himself in the mirror.

And instead, he saw Evelyn looking up at him,
her entire body throbbing with want so clear he felt
it beat against his skin in tidal waves that pulled
him closer and closer. And he'd wanted her with
a kind of feral insanity—the strength of which he
had never experienced before. But he couldn't. She
was innocent. If he hadn't known it before, when he
had first met her in Spain, he knew it now for sure.
It was written in every single part of her body and,
although he'd hated himself for crushing the desire
he so easily read, it was far better than for him to
have toyed with her knowing it would and could not
go any further.

But she was as dangerous to him as he was to her.
She wreaked havoc with his focus and was far too
tangled up in things with his father. No. He needed
to keep her at a safe distance.

He splashed water over his face again, hoping it
would take a bite out of the desire he felt simmering
just beneath the surface of his skin and his civility.

Reaching for a towel, he swiped angrily at his face and threw it aside. He might want to keep a safe distance from her, but he also knew that she would get herself into trouble if she ran off to Indonesia on her own. They just needed to make a plan, he decided as he left the bathroom and made his way back to the suite. He would speak to Evelyn about this and perhaps—

He came to a halt, knowing immediately that she was gone.

Evelyn exited the cab and thanked the driver, turning to gaze up at a train station that looked far more like an airport. Yes, she could have waited until tomorrow for the quicker train. She could even have taken a flight. But she'd needed to go *now*. And not just because she'd stolen from Mateo *again*. Her hands shook as she reached for the strap of her briefcase. She had left with both the octant *and* the notebook, knowing that she would need the notebook when she reached the coordinates and unable to trust Mateo that he would let her have it until then.

She felt faintly sick, but it wasn't because of yet another instance of morally ambiguous behaviour she seemed to engage in since meeting the Spaniard. No. In her mind, she watched as Mateo released his grasp on her chin and stepped back, the apology clear in his gaze. He didn't want her. It was that simple and Evie decided then and there that she'd take disdain over pity any day and she hoped beyond all hope that he'd have the decency to at least let her go.

She made her way into the sprawling international train hub and was thankful that there were signs in English to point her way. She ignored the looks she drew as she rushed through the station, having only had time to grab a handful of clothes and her wash bag before leaving the hotel. She'd not even had time to change.

She found her way to the platform, urgency nipping at her heels. Her heartbeat raced as she boarded the train and found her cabin, an instinct telling her she needed to hurry, while a voice whispered that she was running away.

Of course she was running away, she wanted to cry.

Shame and embarrassment were one thing, but to be rejected like that again... It was too much. It *hurt* too much. She'd tried to pass her encounter off with Jeremy, the boy from Cambridge, as a universal childhood experience. And she'd hoped that the derision and near-exile from her colleagues because of her association with Professor Marin's research would peter out. But it hadn't. Instead, all that rejection and all that hurt had snowballed, accumulating the weight of an avalanche, and she just...she just wanted to breathe.

She put her bags down and sank onto the bottom bunk of the small cabin. It was just big enough for her, with a little table between a small seat on one side and the bunk on the other. A minuscule bathroom was wedged next to the seat and she vowed to change out of her sequinned dress the moment the train left the station. But until then she let the wave of hurt washing over her bring tears to her eyes. Here, alone in the small cabin, she let a few of them go, sweeping them aside with shaking hands before they could fall. She was about to give in completely when a knock pounded against the door. She reached for her ticket and opened the door, only to step back in shock.

'What the hell do you think you're doing?'

Mateo Marin loomed impossibly large in the small doorway, still wearing the tuxedo from the auction earlier that evening. An announcement sounded over the speaker, buzzing in the background, but she couldn't understand it. Her sadness morphed into anger and frustration in a heartbeat. He'd come to stop her because just like everyone else he underestimated her. And she couldn't take it any more.

'I'm following the coordinates. Are you here to stop me? To tell me that you won't "let" me? Please. Tell me that I'm going to "thank you one day",' she challenged him, *dared* him. Something hot and fiery twisted in his gaze.

'You rush off in the middle of the night—'

'It's not even ten pm,' she cut in.

'Without even letting me know—'

'I don't *have* to let you know!' she yelled, her anger rising to unprecedented levels.

'Without a single care for your own safety—'

She huffed out an incredulous laugh. 'Trains are far safer than planes.'

'I wasn't talking about your preferred mode of

transport,' he growled and walked her backwards
into the small cabin. 'You can't just rush out without a plan, having stolen from me *again*. The octant
is mine. The *notebook* is mine. I'm now in this as
much as, if not more than, you. Now, we're getting
off this train and returning to the hotel to figure out
how best to get to these damn coordinates.'

'You want to follow the coordinates?' Evie asked
in surprise.

'Of course I—'

This time it wasn't Evie that interrupted him
but the jerk of the train leaving the station, shoving
her forward and throwing her against his chest. He
reached out a hand to brace it against the overhead
bunk, his other arm wrapping around her, holding
her to him before she could hurt herself.

Instinctively she clung to his waist, her fingers
fisting the black tuxedo jacket, and she could hear
the strong pounding of his heart where her cheek
had landed on his chest. For just a second the wind
lodged in her lungs before coming out on a whoosh.

For a blissful moment he just held her, his hands
firm, his scent intoxicating, but it was the *holding*.
She couldn't remember the last time…*a* time…when
she'd just been *held*.

She heard him curse under his breath and tried
to disentangle herself, embarrassed for weaving a
fantasy from an accident.

'We'll just get off at the next stop,' Mateo said
dismissively.

Evie bit her lip and winced a little.

'What is it?' he demanded.

'Well, it's just that the next stop…' she said, looking into a stormy gaze.

'Yes?'

'It's Hong Kong. In nineteen and a half hours.'

Mateo furiously jabbed out a message to Henri on his phone. He didn't know what he would have to do to make it up to Léi Chen, but he would find a way to do it. Mateo absolutely hated letting people down. In fact, this might just be the first meeting he'd ever missed. Tension and frustration roiled in his gut, and with Evelyn in the bathroom he had nowhere else to direct his ire than into his phone.

He fired off a message to his assistant asking him to arrange for his things to be collected from the hotel and for a car to meet them when they arrived in Hong Kong. Along with his passport. After a rather tense negotiation with the train inspector, he'd been given a fine and forced to buy a ticket for the cabin, although only once the inspector was convinced that Evelyn had no objections.

For a moment, he thought she would object. He'd seen the temptation in her eyes as she glared at him, before finally nodding to the inspector that he could stay in the only free space left on the fully booked train.

He leant back into the small seating square beside the cupboard posing as a bathroom, wincing as his shoulders hit the sides, and mulishly glared at the two bunks on the opposite wall. The top bunk had yellow tape across it, with what he presumed was Chinese for 'out of order'. Hence why the inspector had needed Evie's permission. He rubbed his eyes. His contacts had become dry and were already hurting. By the morning he would be in agony.

Only one bed.

Of course there was only one bed.

The thud of the water shutting off in the cubicle beside him was the only notice he got before Evelyn emerged from a cloud of steam, having *finally* changed out of the dress that had been designed with the sole purpose of driving him out of his goddamned mind. He blinked, hoping to lubricate the lenses.

She took one look at him and sighed. 'I really am sorry about your meeting. But it's not my fault,' she repeated for the hundredth time.

'Really? If you'd just told me where you were going—'

'Mateo,' she snapped, using what he thought of as her teacher voice, 'I am not prepared to fight over this for the next nineteen and a half hours.'

Which was a shame. Because he wanted to fight about *something*. Anything, rather than the unwanted desire coursing through his veins that had grown exponentially when he'd imagined Evie under jets of hot water.

He blinked again.

She slid onto the bunk to sit opposite him, the small plastic table wedged in between them, and peered at him in an unnervingly analytical way.

She sighed again and reached into her briefcase, rummaging around until she found what she was looking for.

'Here. These should work.'

She thrust a pair of glasses across the table at him.

Mateo stared at them as if they might bite. They were his father's. He shook his head, less in denial and more in confusion.

'You have the same prescription. He told me that once.' She smiled sadly. *'"Blind as bats we are. Both of us,"'* she quoted, getting his father's intonation just right. 'He was always losing them, so I got used to carrying a pair around with me. And when I came out to Shanghai I wanted…' She shook the sentence away with a wave of her hand.

She'd wanted a part of his father there with her, he realised.

He nodded, taking the glasses into his hand. Refusing them would reveal more stubbornness than he was willing to concede. If he'd expected some kind of 'there, I told you so', he'd been wrong. Evelyn was still avoiding his gaze and he was pretty sure he knew why.

'Thank you,' he offered reluctantly.

Evelyn finally brought her eyes to his and accepted his thanks with an equally reluctant nod. She pulled a notebook from her briefcase—her own, not his father's—and she started to make notes in it. Something about it was achingly familiar and utterly strange. He had never met her as his father's assistant, but he could see it so easily. The two of them working together. What she had shared with him in the hotel had given him a much stronger understanding of what his father had been looking for in the search for Isabella. But he wasn't quite sure what was driving Evelyn. She'd clearly identified with Isabella but he didn't quite feel that was the whole truth.

'You said that...' He paused to choose his words carefully. He knew that he was treading on painful and dangerous ground for her, but maybe once he understood her, this insane fascination with her would end. 'You said that my father was the first person who understood you. Your adoptive parents... Carol and Alan...they didn't?'

Her pen paused mid-sentence, and everything about her tensed before she seemed to make herself relax with some effort. The table was barely a foot wide and this close he could see every flicker in her eyes, reminding him of embers in a fire. He saw her debate whether to answer him or not and then saw the end of the fight.

'No, I don't think they ever have understood me really. Alan is a retired inventor with several successful patents under his name and Carol is a retired housewife.'

It wasn't that her voice had gone cold, Mateo realised. It was that it had become...clipped. As if compartmentalising as she went. Careful. But there was no warmth, no mess or anecdotes. He felt as if he had been formally introduced to her parents at a cocktail party, without the cocktails or the parents. If he'd been asked about his own mother? He'd probably have complained about a million different things, but all with a smile and all with the knowledge of love, no matter what. That was blisteringly absent from Evie in that moment. And as if by that very absence he heard what they hadn't given her.

'You weren't happy with them?' he asked before he could stop himself.

Evie bit her tongue against the surprising desire to reply honestly. She would always have been truthful, but to be *that*? Honest? About something so personal? The urge was strange and unfamiliar.

'They gave me so much more than I could have ever asked for,' she replied genuinely. 'But they are unaccustomed to...' Torn between loyalty to the people who had taken her in when her birth parents hadn't, and to herself, she simply struggled to find the words for how painful it had been to grow up without the comfort of easy affection. 'They are not the kind of people who eat meals in their kitchen and laugh at daily anecdotes. They are not the kind of people who call weekly and invite you round for dinner at the weekend,' she said, suddenly aware that she was describing things that she'd always wanted from them. 'They care for me, I know that, but showing their feelings isn't something that comes naturally to them,' she said, choosing her words carefully. 'It's not personal to me, because they are the same with everyone.'

'Evelyn, you are not everyone. You are their child,' Mateo insisted gently.

She didn't want to look at him, didn't want to read the sympathy in his eyes that would remind him of his father. The Professor had tried to keep his feelings to himself about her parents, but had often failed spectacularly. The thought softened the hurt radiating out from the bruise she had felt born with, deep in her heart. His defence of her had warmed and soothed in a way she'd never experienced before. But when she did finally meet Mateo's eyes, the fierceness of his gaze, the burning heat of his anger on her behalf made her feel something else entirely. It made her feel *seen*.

'They give me what they are capable of giving and I know and understand that—I know and understand their limits. There simply wasn't any "more" to ask for from them.'

'Did you ever want to look for your birth parents?' he asked hesitantly, as if he was aware he was bashing around the fragile contents of her life and smashing them accidentally.

Evie looked out into the dark beyond the train's window, remembering the sessions she'd had when she was younger with her therapist. Remembering how she'd first been so bewildered by the idea that wanting to be wanted, wanting *love*, wasn't something to be ashamed of. That there wasn't something needy or grabby or desperate within her as she reached again and again for things that weren't there for her. It would have been logical then, perhaps, to search for her birth parents—as Mateo himself had seemed to wonder. But she'd spent years putting words to her feelings and understanding to her emotions, and she'd known then, just as she did now, that she just hadn't been able to face the idea that the people who had given her up for adoption might not want to know her. Might never have regretted their decision. What if, every day, they were thankful that she hadn't reached out to find them? The thought bloomed fresh blood on an old wound and she knew she couldn't risk it. She had stored up her hurt and the room it was locked in was full. There was no more space for her to ache.

Evie exhaled hurt and looked up to find him watching her closely. Instead of answering his question, she asked one of her own. 'Why did you stop speaking to your father?'

His body's reaction was almost imperceptible. Almost. But she'd seen the emotional flinch that had braced his features, the hitch in his breath, the tightening of his shoulders. 'Because I couldn't wait for him any more. I couldn't...' He nodded slowly, understanding and equally unable to put into words the hurt of a child who couldn't trust that they would get what they needed. And it was a need. A need that if not met, it would have been devastating.

'But Evie,' he said, reaching for her hand, laying his over hers in a gesture of comfort that, rather than startling her, she wanted. Welcomed. *Needed.* 'I regret that so much. I regretted it even before you told me about him being at the IPO launch. I regret that I will never get the chance to make peace with him.'

But you still have time, his words whispered.

'You shouldn't let fear hold you back from the things you want to know, Evie.'

She shook her head at his words, as if she could avoid them from finding a painful landing spot on her heart. Avoid the possibility that he might be right. Because…

'If I discovered that my birth parents still didn't want to know me, that they never regretted giving me up for adoption, if their lives are better off without me in it… I don't think… I don't think that I could survive that much rejection,' Evie confessed in the smallest of voices.

When I've already survived so much.

Evie had been so good at pushing aside this hurt, but she suddenly felt it hit her now like a tsunami. It had made her feel vulnerable and ashamed to admit her feelings. And she pushed back at the wave of the other smaller rejections that snowballed in her heart. The boy from Cambridge, the academics that should have supported her. *Him.*

She silently whispered the promise she'd made years ago.

I won't beg to be loved by anyone ever again.

It was a promise that taunted her now as she looked at Mateo, the glasses he wore framing eyes that saw too much and too deeply. But it was precisely the depth of those feelings that made that promise so important even now.

Unable to hold the intensity of his gaze, she looked out of the window. It was late, but they hadn't eaten yet, and even though she wasn't remotely hungry they would need to eat at some point. 'I was going to get some food from the service counter.'

'I'll go,' Mateo offered, getting up quickly, clearly forgetting the tight space he was in, and must have hit the table across his thighs, *hard*, from the wince in his features.

She nodded, not even able to find humour or sympathy in his need to escape. She should be using this time to look at the research on Isabella and Loriella, not in a getting-to-know-you session with Mateo Marin. She barely spared him a glance as he squeezed out into the hallway, her gaze blurred by tears, staring at words she couldn't see, hoping that she could at least hold them back until the door closed behind them.

Mateo cursed himself all the way to the food service counter and back again, ignoring the funny looks he got from his fellow passengers. He should never have asked her that question. And for what? To satisfy his own curiosity? To help shore up his own defences at the expense of hers? That was a low point, even for him. And as much as he hated to admit it, hadn't he already rejected her too? He couldn't lie to himself. He'd seen it in her eyes in the hotel. He'd known what she'd wanted and he'd backed away, and in trying to protect her he'd quite possibly done more harm than good. He prised the door to their cabin open with one hand, while he juggled a mound of unhealthy packaged food in the other, only to discover that Evie had fallen asleep. Head resting upon her arm, which was stretched out across a notebook with a pretty sloping scrawl, she looked serene in comparison to the high emotions that had driven him from the cabin.

He sighed, and sat down beside her. He couldn't leave her like that, she'd feel awful in the morning. He had intended to lift her up and place her properly down on the bunk, but the moment he had her up, she drifted against him and settled there. His only option was to remain like a statue and crick his own neck in the morning, or lean back against the cabin wall and let her sleep against him. His body knew what it wanted, and for the first time since he'd met her, Mateo gave in to the path of least resistance.

He toed his shoes off and, holding her with one arm, managed to slip out of his tuxedo jacket and pull his shirt from his trousers to make himself as comfortable as possible. Giving up, he leaned back against the wall and arranged her as comfortably as possible. Her hand slipped around his waist, while her cheek rested against his chest, and as much as he wished to curse himself to hell and back, he decided that it was the least he deserved. He could undergo a few hours of the sensual torture of having a beautiful woman pressed against him. From here, he could pick out the red and gold strands that took her hair from dull brown towards auburn. Assured that she was asleep, he picked up a lock of the soft threads and ran them between his thumb and forefinger. Smooth and silky.

In his mind, he plunged his fingers through her hair to scrape gently against her scalp and she leaned her head back into his touch, exposing her neck to his lips, and on his tongue he remembered the taste of citrus and heat and...

Cristo, what was he thinking? Not only was she so clearly innocent, but she was also vulnerable on a deep emotional level thanks to the very people who should have protected her. It angered and infuriated him in a way that made a mockery of his desire and need for her.

She stirred beneath him and he quietly cleared his throat, the sound cutting through the small cabin. He forced his frustration to the back of his mind, and without moving her too much reached for the notebook Evelyn had been reading. He supposed if he was to go on a treasure hunt, he should at least try to be prepared.

He peered at the notebook held in one hand through the glasses she'd given him. She'd been right. They were a match for his prescription and he hadn't even known that. As he read through her notes, he saw the questions scribbled in the margins about what his father would think, whether he would have seen it the same way as she did. And in his mind, he saw a student missing her mentor, finding her own path and making her own discoveries, but alone in those discoveries with absolutely no support from the academic world. And even as his conscience stirred, she nestled deeper against him.

Evie fisted her hand in the cotton sheet as she began to wake. Her felt heart bruised and raw but that was background to something much more persistent in her mind and body. Heat surrounded her, and the scent that filled her senses was woodsy and salty, sharp with a bite of bay. She remembered that scent, but couldn't quite place it in her half-asleep state. Desire crawled across her skin, heat slipped between her heartbeats and need throbbed between her thighs. She shifted her legs in an attempt to soothe the ache and stopped when she felt the superfine wool of a man's trousers. Not just *a* man. *Mateo.*

Her eyes sprang open to find her hand fisted in the cotton of his shirt, her other hand wedged between her cheek and his chest. Frozen still, she felt a gentle press against the back of her head, and in the reflection of the cabin's window she realised she was lying practically on top of Mateo, his hand pressed against her head in an almost possessive way. She bit her lip to stop herself from moving, terrified he might wake to find her draped all over him.

His head faced the other way to her, his chin angled down towards the top of her head. His glasses were on the tip of his finger, dangling from his free hand, hanging off the side of the bed and hovering above her notebook that was now on the floor. She must have fallen asleep at the table, she realised. Not that it explained how she was currently sprawled across him.

The sound of his heart thudded in her ear again, slow, powerful and unstoppable. That was what he made her think of, that was what he was like; powerful and unstoppable. She was fascinated by that kind of force, that kind of self-assurance. She had tasted a hint of it in the moments before he kissed her in his bedroom, before he'd discovered who she was. A hint that had remained in the back of her mind like a drug, one she wanted again. Even now her breath caught in her lungs, pressing her chest against his side, arousal and want hardening her nipples to painful points that only he could appease…and never would. Because instead of erotic fantasies, she remembered the way he had pulled back from her in the hotel, apologies in his eyes and barriers between them. And if she continued to lie there indulging in silly schoolgirl fantasies she would only hurt herself more. He stirred beneath her, his free arm coming up from where it had dangled off the bed, to wrap around her and hold her in place.

In her shock she squeaked, but he mumbled at her to go back to sleep. And she wanted to. She wanted to go to sleep with someone holding her tight, wrapped in a warm heat and the unspoken promise of what could happen when she woke. But she couldn't. Because at that precise moment, the train began to slow.

'What's going on?' a sleep-fogged voice asked from beneath her.

'We're here,' she answered.

CHAPTER SEVEN

THE CAR MATEO'S assistant had arranged to meet them from the station in Hong Kong took them to a small private airport where Evie's benefactor had arranged for a small flight to take them out to Amahai Airport on Maluku. From there, further 'transport' would take them to the coordinates. Transport turned out to be a one-hundred-and-five-foot yacht with a twin engine, a Jacuzzi, three impressive suites, with a galley and staff accommodation, worth more than he'd just paid for the octant.

'You need a plan, Evelyn,' he argued, standing on the jetty beside the exquisite boat that gleamed in the morning sun.

'I have one,' she said, passing her briefcase to a young woman in a white uniform.

'Really?'

'Yes, this boat will take me to the island the coordinates pinpoint.'

'An *uninhabited* island, buried deep in the Kei Islands. What if the weather is bad?'

'The yacht has state-of-the-art stabilisers, sir,'

the woman in the white uniform informed him. He glared at her in thanks—she was *not* helping.

'Why are you making this so difficult?' Evie asked.

'Because for a genius, you are not thinking this through. You need a base of operations. You need to do your research, gather your information and then go to the site.'

'You sound a lot like your father at the moment.'

'Said no one ever,' he growled.

Evelyn sighed. 'This will be my base of operations. We will dock…moor, berth—?'

'Drop anchor, ma'am,' clarified the woman in the white uniform.

'Thank you,' Evelyn said. 'Drop anchor as near to the coordinates as possible and I'll assess from there.'

Mateo glared out at the sea.

'Tell me,' she asked, 'when you muscled your way onto a journey that, for me, has been almost twenty years in the making, and for you twenty-four hours, did you think that you would suddenly be in charge?'

'What? Absolutely not,' he replied, disliking the transparency of his thoughts.

'Okay, then. I'm sorry you got stuck on a train here with me, and I'm sorry you missed your very important meeting—'

Her words stopped short as he closed the distance between them with a single step. He leaned into her space, not to intimidate but to make his point completely clear. And if his whole body felt on fire being this close to the woman who had slept with him, *on him*, for the last eight hours, then he ruthlessly ignored it. Only it wasn't so easy to cast aside the flare of desire he saw burst to life in her eyes.

'I'm coming with you,' he said, determined to see this through.

'Well—'

'And you are forgetting the most important thing, of course. That it is *mine*,' he said, plucking the leather notebook carefully from her grasp, and stalking past Evelyn, and up the ramp onto the yacht, ignoring all the alarms going off in his head.

He strode down the steps that led him to the lower salon, through polished wood, luxurious leather, and opulence towards the captain, who stood outside a fairly impressive cabin with ten windows.

'Ms Edwards suggested you sleep here while on board,' the uniformed man said before disappearing.

Mateo threw his suitcase angrily onto the bed. Why was he so annoyed that she was trying to get rid of him? His ego was healthy enough to survive it even if he'd taken it to heart, but that wasn't it. And no, he was not concerned about following her lead in this—it *was* her world, she had the knowledge and the experience here. But he was invested too. And not just because he wanted to validate his father's legacy, he wanted to validate *hers*. He wanted all the academics who had turned their back on her to know that they had been wrong to do so. The urge was so strong and so urgent, he had completely forgotten to check in with Henri about Léi Chen.

* * *

Having taken the hour since they'd left the dock to freshen up and change into new clothes, Evie arrived for lunch at the upper salon to find a beautifully set table covered in a crisp white table-cloth. She'd felt a little awkward unpacking the clothes that Mateo's assistant had, surprisingly, procured for her, worried about the size and style. But whether he was redeeming himself or had a very good eye, she was eternally thankful. There were enough clothes for a week packed into the brand-new case, along with the kind of clothes she would happily wear for her field work. But it was the ankle-length green dress with twisted straps that she loved the most. It clung to her chest and waist and fell from her hips, making her feel feminine and pretty. She had paired them with the other thing in the suitcase that had made her smile—a pair of wedged sandals. Just one of the pairs of heeled shoes and sandals that she would have bought for herself. As she turned to check her reflection in the mirror, the press of the material against her waist reminded her of Mateo's hand wrapping around her to hold her against him. Her heart leapt, skin warmed, and once again she felt breathless with want. She would have changed out of it, if it hadn't been for the fact that lunch was waiting on her. And now, as she walked towards the table, the dress leaving her bare skin cool in the warm breeze, she told herself not to hope for some kind of reaction from him.

The man in question leant against the railings

at the bow, looking out at the horizon. She hadn't thought he could look any more impressive than when he'd been in a tux, but dressed in tan linen trousers and white shirt he was lethal. Wind came off the South China Sea and ruffled the heavy, lazy curls of his hair.

Her gaze was drawn to the breadth of his shoulders, wide and strong, and she let the desire to be surrounded by those shoulders drift away on the breeze. And once she had let go of that want, she noticed how stiffly he held himself, as if he were weighed down. She remembered the Professor getting this way when he couldn't get what he wanted. Evie nearly smiled. It had always reminded her, somewhat, of a slightly stroppy child. And while there was nothing childlike about Mateo, it was fascinating to see that, despite their estrangement, there were similarities that could only have been hereditary. Before the thought could take her on a tangent as to what characteristics she might have inherited, she thought back to her earlier accusation. She had meant what she said earlier about him muscling his way onto this journey with her, but secretly…she was pleased. Not just because he was the Professor's son, but because of him. The last two years had been quiet and…lonely, she was beginning to realise.

Evie reached the table where Annie, the steward who had met them on the jetty, filled two glasses with a chilled white wine before retreating to leave them alone.

Evie felt, rather than saw, Mateo's attention turn

to her, as if he had run a palm down the outside of her arm. Goosebumps followed the imaginary caress perusing her body like a forbidden touch. Did he know the effect he had on her? Surely he wouldn't be so cruel as to taunt her in such a way, especially having rejected her at the hotel? Frustration dampened her desire. Despite the promise she'd made, she found herself vehemently wanting someone who didn't want her back.

Willing back the wave of emotion that swelled as strongly as the sea beneath the boat, she took a seat at the table and faced a selection of incredible fish—cured, seared, roasted from the look of it—even though any hunger fled the moment that Mateo sat opposite her. If Mateo had looked good against the bow, he looked almost devastating up close. Her pulse flared at his proximity, as if it was responding to some silent call from him, and heat inched across her skin like a trail of fire. Ordering herself to snap out of it, she focused on the job she was here to do. The Queen had decided not to tell her father about the coordinates found in the octant until Evie had been able to assess the situation. Once they knew what they were dealing with, further decisions could be made. And now, here, finally she allowed herself to feel that thread of professional excitement. The hope that they might finally find proof of what the Professor had searched so long and so hard for.

But what are you *looking for?*

Evie looked up to find that Mateo was holding

out her glass of wine to her and she took it, careful to avoid even the most accidental of touches.

'What do you think we'll find?' he asked, sitting back in his chair, apparently content to sip at his wine for the moment. She could feel the sense of determination about him now that he'd decided to join her in following the clues left in the octant. It seemed to have refined his features, given everything focus and clarity. And she wished it hadn't, because it made him seem even *more*.

'At the island? I have no idea,' she confessed, following his lead and taking a sip of the delicious wine. Perhs she would find her hunger again in a moment. 'I'm hoping for a ducatoon, stiver or guilder—coins used by the Dutch East India Company. If we're really lucky, maybe some jewellery that could be linked to someone specific.'

'You're hoping for so little?'

'Little,' she repeated incredulously. 'That would be *huge*. It's not like it is in the movies, Mateo. You don't just stumble across a chest of buried treasure.'

'Or a pirate ship,' he added.

Evie smiled reluctantly. 'Or a pirate ship. I honestly can't imagine that there will be much to find after more than four hundred years. Surely anything to find would have been found by now, so to find even *something* would be incredible.'

'You're excited,' he observed.

'Yes, aren't you?' she asked him, as if incredulous that he might not be.

Mateo wished he could tell her truthfully that he wasn't. But in that moment, he did feel it. Rushing through his veins a strange lightness, coursing through him, making him *hopeful*. He could see it though, that bright, open excitement in her eyes that reminded him of his father.

'You're just like him,' he said, the words falling from his lips before he could call them back. But he meant them. He remembered the almost childish joy his father would express, infectious and thrilling, so that when Mateo would listen to his father's stories of pirate princesses and the legendary Dutch East India Company, Mateo wanted to go with him. As a child, he'd dreamed of hunting treasure and sword fights and laughing as he played with a father who indulged his imagination with history tempered with a little bit of fairy-tale.

'If you *could* find anything, what would it be?' he asked, wanting to see just a little more of her when she was like this. Wanting to see a little more of his father.

'I would like to find just some sense of them,' she replied instantly, utterly unguarded.

'Them?' he questioned, not sure what Evie was talking about.

She blinked as if she'd only just realised what she'd said and sat back a little as if to distance herself from what she'd revealed.

'Evie?' Her name called her back to his question.

'I think Loriella and her first mate were married,' she explained.

'I don't remember my father ever talking about that.'

'He didn't…it wasn't his theory,' she confessed.

'It's *yours*,' Mateo stated.

'Yes.'

He stared at her patiently, daring her to tell him her theory about Isabella.

'You don't know what you're asking,' she said to him, a plea in her voice he chose to ignore. She shook her head as if she could shake him off. 'I've been ridiculed enough just aiding Professor Marin's research. A female archaeologist, following such a romantic, unproveable legend? I would never work again.'

She reached for her glass and took a sip of wine.

'It's just me, here,' he said, suddenly convinced that this was the most important thing he could know about her.

She sighed, and he wondered if she realised that she was looking out over the same sea that she believed Princess Isabella to have sailed, to have waged a war against her ex-fiancé, against the injustices the Dutch East India Company were committing.

'I believe that after Princess Isabella survived the attack on her ship, she became close to the first mate, who taught her everything she needed to know. I believe that she proved herself to him and to the crew and that the change of her name was intended to show that she was more loyal to them than her own family. I believe that rumours were spread to denigrate her and destroy her spirit and she didn't let them.'

He wondered if she could see it, the parallels that had consciously or otherwise drawn Evie to Isabella. Because how could she not see that the strength she admired in the Pirate Princess was the same strength she showed every single day against the colleagues who had turned their backs on her, or the family that had abandoned her? 'You admire her,' he stated.

'Absolutely. When she had been left for dead by everyone she knew, instead of giving up, she pushed on—overcoming an incredible amount to lead some of the most dangerous mercenaries in the world at that time. And it led her to a man who respected her, rather than resenting her gender or inexperience. A man who followed her rather than taking a lead that would have pretty much been his right to take as First Mate. But instead he brought her into his life, he shared that with her, supporting her and letting her shine. It was a true partnership.'

He heard the yearning in her voice, added it to the bits and pieces she'd shared with him about her life. Mateo's heart thudded once, heavily. A cloud passed in front of the sun, the cool descending over the table as if she'd reached out with her cold hands and touched him.

He could see it in her eyes. The wistfulness, the hope. And it dawned on him that Evelyn wanted something that was as far removed from what he could even begin to imagine from himself. A chasm opened up between them and, somehow, she felt it happen too.

'Mateo?'

'It's nothing,' he dismissed.

'It's clearly not nothing,' she said, frowning at him as if trying to see what he was thinking.

He looked up at her and realised that she might have misunderstood. 'No, Evelyn, I... There is nothing to be embarrassed or concerned about with your theory of Loriella and her husband, if that was what he was.' He'd hate to think that he had offered her a safe space to share her thoughts and then taken that space away. But... He shook his head. 'I just... I just don't think those kinds of partnerships are real or lasting. I think that what you're looking for in Isabella and her first mate are as much fantasy as—'

'As the treasure?' she demanded, the warning signs of an angry flush painting her delicate cheeks.

'No, I just think it's naïve to—'

'Naïve?'

Cristo. He was getting this wrong, but he was frustrated, annoyed by her outrage. Because he had seen what happened when those once-in-a-lifetime loves went wrong. Wasn't that precisely what had happened to his parents? An age-old anger rose, unfurling and twisting, adding heat and hurt to words he could barely stop himself from saying.

'Yes, naïve,' he said, shaking his head. 'My mother believed in that kind of marriage, that kind of partnership, and what did it get her? Nothing.

Nothing but crying herself to sleep every single night for a year after we returned to Spain. Nothing but having to start over again under the pitying, watchful gaze of a family who had never thought she should marry an English academic anyway. Of having to pretend that everything was okay, when inside she was being torn apart. But do you know what the real kicker is? Why she actually left him? It wasn't because she didn't love him,' he said, sounding as surprised as he'd always felt. 'It wasn't because she didn't want to be with him. It was because of *me*. It was because she couldn't bear to see me disappointed every single time my father would forget a birthday, or a celebratory meal, or that he'd promised to read me a book that evening, or that he'd promised to attend my graduation. So, if that's what partnership and true love get you? I'll take a hard pass, thank you.'

'Mateo…' Evelyn reached across the table, but he pulled his hand away, unable to put the roiling mass of emotions back into the box he usually kept them safely locked away in.

'Do you know what? I honestly don't know one single marriage that has lasted. Henri's mother raised him by herself, even my board of governors has two failed marriages behind it and one impending divorce between them.'

'Carol and Alan are still married,' she pointed out.

'And what a fine bastion of the institution of love and affection they are,' he snapped, watching as she flushed pink and then pale, so pale as the blood ran from her cheeks. Guilt fisted his chest. 'Evie, I'm—'

She stumbled up from the chair and he cursed, seeing the tears that gathered in her eyes. 'If you'll excuse me, I…' Without finding the words to finish that sentence she disappeared and he damned himself to hell and back. He hadn't meant to upset her. Why was he getting everything wrong when it came to her?

Three hours later, Evie stared out of the window of her cabin, her eyes a little less puffy than they had been before. The conversation with Mateo had been painful, but more so for him than for her, she'd decided. Yes, what he'd said about Carol and Alan had cut, but she could hardly say that it wasn't true.

It was the glimpse of the little boy who had been so badly hurt by the breakdown of his parents' relationship that had clutched at her heart. A little boy who had taken responsibility for something not of his own making. She could see it so easily. A mother who had tried, but failed, to hide her pain from her son. A father who had been so distraught by the breakdown of his marriage, he'd buried himself in his work. And Mateo… Mateo, who had closed himself off from the one thing that might have healed his wounds.

She let a sad laugh escape as she imagined Mateo's sardonic response to that observation.

And what have you closed yourself off to?

Everything.

The response was immediate and sounded so

very much like her childhood voice that it shocked
Evie. The instinctive reply screamed in her mind as
she recognised how again and again she had pulled
herself back from things and people that might re-
ject her. Might cause her hurt. What if Mateo was
right and she *had* let fear hold her back from what
she wanted? What if she had stopped looking for the
truth about Isabella because she was worried about
doing even more harm to her reputation? What if
she had held herself back from the possibility of a
relationship with her birth parents because she was
fearful of their rejection? What if she was doing it
even now, with Mateo? Holding herself back because…because…?

A knock sounded on the door, interrupting her
thoughts and, thinking it was Annie coming to take
away the tea tray she'd ordered to her room earlier,
she called out, 'Come in.'

The door opened and Mateo stood there, filling
the frame with the breadth of his shoulders, looking
for all the world like a rakish seducer. His shirt was
undone at the neck, sleeves rolled back, his hands
fisted in his pockets, hair mussed and tousled and
something unreadable in his gaze.

Oh, *why* did he have to make her heart pound like
that? Why did he have to make her *want* so much?

'I came to apologise.'

His eyes were clear from the storm that she had
seen earlier at the table on the deck. The bronze
depths sparking with truth.

'You don't need to,' she said a little more sharply than she had intended.

'I belittled your feelings,' he admitted.

'And I underestimated yours,' she replied.

He nodded, acknowledging the truth of her words. 'Still, I shouldn't have said what I said about Carol and Alan.'

'Thank you. I appreciate that.'

'I also wanted to let you know that we'll be dropping anchor shortly.'

'Why? Are we there already?' she asked, eagerness and excitement a flashover through her body.

'No,' Mateo said, shaking his head. 'But we've arrived at Kei Island and I've booked us suites there for tonight.'

'Why? We need to push on to the coordinates, Mateo.'

He held his hand up. 'Evie.' Her name was almost a plea, making her waver in her determination to keep the distance she needed between them. 'Let's take this evening and get our feet back beneath us. Tomorrow could throw anything at us.'

It was so tempting. To take a pause in the storm of emotions swirling in her heart. But she wasn't sure that being even closer to Mateo was what she needed right now.

'What about the yacht's staff?'

'They'll remain on board.'

'I still think I should stay…' she hedged.

He held up his hands as if in surrender. 'If that's what you want…'

He had turned regretfully away, but something about the words he'd used...

If that's what you want.

'Wait,' she called after him, and this time when he turned she couldn't help but return his infectious smile.

Evie didn't know what she had expected from the island that Annie had taken Mateo and her to on the yacht's small speedboat. After a day at sea, with nothing but the blue sky and daydreams of pirate ships, she'd been surprised by the hustle and bustle of an island so clearly dedicated to upmarket tourism.

They'd bypassed the marina, where yachts matched or even surpassed the upscale boats she'd seen in Hong Kong, and disembarked at a much smaller wooden jetty, empty of people or boats. Mateo had held out his hand to help her off the boat, and she'd ignored the zap of electricity that had arced from his touch.

He had waved Annie off as she turned the boat back to the ship and led Evie confidently up the jetty to a thicket of palm trees and green vegetation. The sun was beginning to set and the entire island was painted in a soft yellow glow that was beginning to burn red at the edges. And when Mateo looked back over his shoulder to check she was still with him, she half fancied she had been touched by its rays.

She had packed some overnight things in her briefcase, along with her notebook and the Professor's, and as she looked around she felt at peace for the first time in a long time. It was something that settled into her skin and sank into her bones. The call to relax, the urge to let go a little, and she thought she'd seen the same thing in Mateo's eyes. The wooden jetty turned into a path that cut into the grove of palm trees and she was about to ask Mateo where they were going when the trees opened up and she stepped almost directly onto a beach of pure white sand, the likes of which she'd only ever experienced in her wildest fantasies.

She couldn't help the gasp that fell from her lips as she took in the curve of the sandy bay and the azure-blue sea gently lapping rhythmically at the blond grains of the beach. Halfway across the bay, widely interspersed between palm trees, were four huts, open to the elements, with thatched roofs and string lights hanging from the eves.

There wasn't another soul on the beach and something unfurled in her chest as excitement and hope lifted the lid on her desires. She dared to cast her gaze to Mateo, praying not to find disinterest or boredom in something that was so magical to her, but she should have known better.

Because there, looking back at her with the same sense of barely repressed excitement, was Mateo, and the words next on his lips stole her heart.

'Welcome to paradise.'

CHAPTER EIGHT

ONCE AGAIN MATEO found himself marvelling at how expressive Evie's face was. He could have described every single feeling she experienced as she looked out across the beach at dusk. But wonder was the one he recognised the most. That was what he'd wanted when he'd asked Annie to let them off here at one of the Kei Islands. To take away the hurt he'd carelessly inflicted and cover it with something beautiful.

There was a much larger hotel on the other side of the island, but this? This was perfect. He had no intention of telling her that he'd hired out the entire hotel for just the two of them. He bit back a laugh at the thought of how she would berate him for the waste of money. But he didn't consider it a waste at all.

He'd bitterly regretted the things he'd said over lunch. It didn't mean that he'd changed his feelings about it, but he should never have said what he'd said, nor spoken of her adoptive parents. If he was honest with himself, he knew where his anger came from, a deep realisation of what they could never be to each other; of what they could never have. But he also knew that he'd have to make it up to her. And from the look on her face, he was right. Something hot and heavy eased in his chest and he breathed his first full breath since that afternoon.

'Dinner will be served on the beach in an hour, but until then you can get settled in your suite, or you can take a swim, or...' The way she was looking at him stopped his words. 'What?'

'I'm not quite sure that this is how I'd describe getting my feet back under me. It's more like sweeping me off them,' she half laughed, but stopped suddenly as if she'd realised what she'd said. She bit her lip as his gut clenched, but then... 'Thank you,' she said, simply. For a moment he thought she was going to rise on her toes and press a kiss to his cheek. For a moment he *wanted* that. But then she was gone, walking past him towards the huts in the apex of the bay.

Walk away. Walk away now.

A familiar internal warning ran through his brain, and for the first time since he could remember he wanted to ignore it. He followed behind her, trying to ignore the allure of the sway of her hips and the way that her wedged sandals sank her a little lower into the sand. He kept pace with her until she came to a stop a few feet away from the huts, sensing her reluctance to tear herself away from the view of the sea.

That he was just as reluctant to tear himself away from the view of her was all he needed to know that he should find his suite before he did something he couldn't take back. Maybe he was the one who should have stayed back on the yacht, not Annie.

Evie remembered telling Queen Sofia that she had never stayed anywhere more beautiful, but this? Mateo wasn't wrong. It really was paradise. She looked around her at the achingly stunning sur-roundings. It felt like serenity and she hadn't re-alised how much she'd needed it. The hut Mateo had pointed her to was on one side of the beach, his was at the far end of the small settlements. She'd known that because she'd all but hidden behind a curtain and watched as he'd walked to the far side of the encampment and up the steps of a hut that mirrored hers, half thankful and half bereft for the distance between them.

The front of the exotic suite faced the sea and was open to the elements. Even now a gentle salt-scented breeze pushed at the tendrils of hair that escaped the loose plait she'd wound her hair into. Behind her, a series of reed walls allowed both for a sense of lib-erating openness and discreet privacy. The bath-room was enclosed, and there was a shower out on the decking that wrapped around the hut completely hidden from view.

A canopy bed was placed in the centre of the hut with views of a beach now dusted with dusk and from which she could already see a few twinkling stars in the sky. She had seen a few people dressed in white and black uniforms discreetly passing before the huts, presumably getting their dinner together.

It served only to remind her of the night she had met Mateo. Had it really only been three days ago? Before, when she'd thought of the Professor's son, there had been resentment towards an undefinable figure who, in her mind, had taken his father for granted. But now? Now that she had seen so much more in the *man,* could she really continue to lie to herself and deny that she wanted him? That, even knowing he didn't want the love and marriage she secretly was so hopeful she would have in her own life, she *still* wanted him?

She was almost sure that he desired her—she felt it press against her when he looked at her, burn in her skin when he touched her, fill her lungs whenever he was near—but it was clear that he didn't *want* to want her. Something in her fought against that, wanted to push and prod and poke at the barrier between them.

They had clashed from the very first moment they'd met, and in that fire, in that friction, was something alive and twisting, needing to get out. It simmered beneath her skin, making her restless, making her...*reckless*. Never before had she understood more the phrase 'throwing caution to the wind'. The thoughts and hope for her future, they belonged to someone else, to some other time. He had brought her to paradise and it was whispering desires and wants from her most secret fantasies.

Could she really just ask him for what she wanted?

Could she take just this night, perhaps?

There was something seductive in the thought of just one night. Not because he might agree, but because surely, if she knew that there was no possibility of the kind of future she wanted, then she would be safe from hurt? Her *heart* would be safe?

She started at the gentle tinkle of a bell. Frowning, she made her way out onto the decking and the sight made her heart leap. A wooden dais had appeared as if by magic. Large fire torches marked each corner, illuminating a white cloth-covered table set for a feast and decorated with local flowers and shells. Mateo was standing in front of it, waiting expectantly for her.

She was thankful she'd taken the time to freshen up and change into the sarong that had been waiting for her on the bed. The material was soothing against her heated skin and the colour, a deep turquoise, was beautiful. She'd never worn anything like it, but when Mateo's eyes finished his slow, intense perusal from top to toe, returning to meet her gaze, she felt absolutely incredible—invincible almost. It was only when she took the first step onto the sandy beach that she realised she had left her heels behind, and, barefoot, she made her way towards him with a self-confidence that was empowering. Her heart shifted in her chest as she drew level with Mateo, who hadn't taken his eyes off her once.

'You are beautiful,' he said, the words not intended to flatter, or to manipulate. It was simply a fact for him, but she wanted more. They fired something in her breast, as if they had been a call to arms that only she heard. He poured her a glass of wine and passed it to her.

'Where are the other guests?' Evie asked.

'It's just us tonight,' he replied, trying to swallow the heat in his throat.

The table was full of lots of little dishes, all of which he was sure were utterly delicious, but Mateo couldn't have described a single one. He was simply unable to draw his attention away from Evie. As if by tacit agreement, they avoided speaking of the Professor or the coordinates, but instead shared happy stories of their childhoods. Over the starter, Mateo dutifully described the trouble he would get into at boarding school with Henri. He couldn't have said when the plates were cleared, because of the way her eyes shimmered at hearing about his achievements and his own sense of accomplishment at providing his mother and friends with the security he felt they deserved. He barely noticed the main course as Evie regaled him with amusingly awkward stories of Carol and Alan, and through dessert, she entertained him with the more humorous disasters she'd experienced as a young girl as she'd tried to navigate her intelligence in an environment meant for much older children.

'Do you feel you missed out on things?'

'Absolutely,' she said, nodding. 'I was tutored at home until I was sixteen and then went straight to university. All of the normal experiences you had with Henri—'

'I'm not sure I'd call them normal,' Mateo laughingly interrupted.

'Maybe not,' she conceded with a smile, 'but things like school dances, or walking home with friends, or sharing gossip and crushes on the cool boys...' Her breath shuddered in her chest, just a little, just enough for him to hear the longing for things she hadn't had or known. When she looked up at him from across the table, he suddenly realised that they had wandered into dangerous territory. Because the way she looked at him pulled his pulse into a faster beat, it filled the air between them with a heavy sensuality and everything in him wanted to respond to it—a siren's call that would dash them both on the rocks if they were not careful.

'There are things that I—'

'Evie.' Her name was a plea on his tongue, needing her to stop. He'd seen so much of her in the last few days. Not just his father's assistant, or a woman determined to follow an ancient treasure hunt. But also the woman she was...incredible, powerful, proud, intelligent. He admired her. And he didn't want to hurt her. He didn't want to give her false promises of a future he had no intention or ability to offer her.

She bit her lip, and once again he regretted dimming that light, thinking wrongly that it had been extinguished. But when she looked back up at him,

anger shimmering with desire, he realised the spark
had been lit and now threatened to *burn*.

'There are things that I want,' she repeated, her
voice trembling a little, but no less clear for it. Her
determination pushed him to the brink. Everything
in him warred between walking away and pulling
her to him.

He started, when she pushed her chair back and
stood, slowly coming around the table, her bare feet
sandy and soft on the wooden platform.

'There are things that I want and if I don't say it
now, I...' She paused and he thought he understood.
He expected that she might not find the courage
again, but he was wrong. He had underestimated
her again, and that would be the last time he would
ever do it. 'If I don't say it now, I will be smaller. I
will be less. And I don't want to be less. I want to be
as strong as Isabella was when she faced down the
pirate that attacked her ship. I want to be as fierce
as she was when she defended her crew against her
fiancé. So I know that you might turn me away,
but,' she let out a small laugh, 'this actually isn't
about you. It's about me,' she said. And as if realising the truth of her words as she spoke them, she
shone. Her eyes sparkled and her skin glowed beneath a milky moon.

He stood to take her hand, gazing into all that
was her glory.

'I'm listening.'

'I want you to kiss me,' she said, and heat burned
his lungs on an inhale. 'I want you to crush my

lips to yours and fill my mouth with your tongue.'
Her words were an erotic fantasy, the imagery of
it, slashing red marks across his cheeks. 'I want to
taste you,' she said, 'and I want you to taste me,'
the soft wishes morphing into something hot and
carnal. 'I want you to touch me, to cover my body
with your hands.'

Evelyn's breath was coming in pants he could feel
against his lips. *Cristo*, it was taking every single
ounce of strength to hold himself back.

'I want you to touch me in places that will make
me moan with pleasure,' she said, as heat and need
built in his chest until he thought he might explode.
'I want you to relieve the ache burning across my
body and delight in doing it,' she all but begged.

'And I know,' she said as he opened his mouth to
speak, 'I know it wouldn't be more than tonight. But
just for tonight, I want that,' Evie said, her hands
bunching the beautiful turquoise material at her
thighs, as he bit back a moan of need so strong he
wanted to tear the world apart.

'And I wanted you to know that,' she said before
turning away.

Before she could take a step, he reached for her
wrist and drew her back, pulling her against the
length of his body, relishing in finally, *finally*, having her against his skin. With one hand he cupped
her jaw as the other pressed her against him.

'You wanted to be as strong as Isabella?' he
asked.

She nodded, trying to avoid his gaze.

'How did you not know that you already are?' he asked, searching her eyes for an answer he wasn't sure he didn't already know. And, unable to deny them both what they so desperately wanted, he claimed her lips with his.

Her mouth parted on a cry, as he hoped it would, opening for him, welcoming his passion. Her hands threaded through his hair, holding him to her as if she was worried he might disappear. He cradled her neck in the palm of his hand, half terrified of exactly the same thing. An urgency overwhelmed him even as he gentled his desire, remembering her innocence and inexperience. He wouldn't turn away from her, not unless she asked it, but he knew that he should ease back a little. He slowed the kiss, closing it with a careful bite of her bottom lip.

'I know you want those things, and I know that you've thought it through, in here,' he said, tapping gently at her temple. 'But what you feel in here,' he said, pausing to lay his palm against her chest, 'might be different to what you expect.'

'If you're asking me—'

He cut her words off with a kiss, lips pulled into a slight curve by his smile from the indignance in her tone. 'Evie,' he said, resting his forehead against hers, 'I'm not asking if you've changed your mind. But I have to make sure you understand that I cannot offer you more than this,' he said, searching her level gaze, thankful she clearly had no idea of the storm raging within him. She had offered him everything he had wanted from her and for her and only the thinnest thread of selflessness was holding him back. But it was strong enough. Because he needed her to know that he could not be what he knew was in her dreams. 'I cannot give you forever and happy-ever-after, Evie. It's just not in me.'

Solemn eyes stared back at him, green and gold flickers in the hazel-brown depths.

'I understand,' she said sincerely, and half of him urged, now! Now! But that thread still held him back, so very careful of her inexperience.

'I want you to know that if you want to stop at any point, I'll stop. If you think it's too far, or even if you just need a moment, I'll stop and it won't change a thing between us. I need you to know that.'

It was as if a hand had swept aside all the obstacles muddying the waters between them. In that moment, Evie understood him perfectly and she felt understood completely. Trust. That was what it was. She trusted herself with him utterly and irrevocably and he trusted that she would be true to herself with him. It spoke to her soul in a way that made Mateo's words true. She didn't know what to expect to feel from this...but everything in her wanted to find out.

She rose onto her toes and pressed a chaste kiss against his lips, once, then twice. By the third, her tongue swept out to taste his lip, then his mouth, and then...oh, then it was heaven. As he opened for her, he pulled her into him, his arms sweeping around her as his tongue filled her mouth and she felt possessed. Not owned, but joined. Her skin ached and the juncture of her thighs throbbed with want. Her

legs became restless, and just when they began to
tremble he swept her up into his arms, and without
breaking the kiss he walked them to his cabin, up
the wooden steps, and into a suite that mirrored hers.

He placed her on the end of the canopied bed
and she barely spared a glance for the hundreds
of tea lights glittering around the cabin. With the
night sky in the distance and the shimmering can-
dles around them, she felt as if she were on a bed
amongst the stars.

He stood before her, slowly undoing the buttons
of his linen shirt, his eyes not once moving from
her. She bit her lip, aching at the sight of him. Intellectually she didn't quite understand her reaction to him, but instinctively she knew that it was
unique. That she had never, would never feel the
same way again. Because it wasn't just the breadth
of his shoulders, the defined musculature, the dust-
ing of dark hair that whispered the word *man* in her
heart and soul, it was him.

She lost herself in the heady sense of power arc-
ing between them, being passed back and forth and
shared in a way she could hardly put into words. She
raised her hands to release the tie of the sarong at
her neck, wanting to be as naked as he, and just as
he shrugged out of the shirt, the silky material fell
from around her neck to her waist, leaving her top
half completely bare to his perusal.

Something powerful and feminine soared at the
heat slashing his cheeks and the sparks of ferocious
need in his gaze. And she, who had spent years

feeling shame and fearing embarrassment, felt almost invincible. He prowled towards her, forcing her back, even as she felt in control. He leaned over her as she lay against the large bed until he covered her body with his own.

'Evie, if I'd known that you were naked beneath the ties of your sarong,' he whispered against her neck as he placed upon it little kisses that showered her skin in goosebumps, 'we wouldn't have eaten a thing. You are so utterly beautiful,' he said, and she wondered if he'd realised that he'd slipped into Spanish.

His hand smoothed across the skin of her side, skating perilously close to where she wanted him to cup her breast, the gentleness of his touch beginning to grate, offering only a taste of what she truly wanted. Him, unfettered, and as lost to passion as she. But when his hand curved her hip and slipped beneath the material that had rucked up beneath her, her heart leapt with want. Her pulse pounded so hard in her chest, she half imagined he could hear it.

His fingers dug in, not so gentle now, and she almost came off the bed, desperately pressing her chest against his, wanting relief, needing release. His hands swept around her thigh and gently parted her legs beneath him. He had barely touched her and she was sobbing with need.

Back and forth he soothed the sensitive skin of her thigh, before he slipped his fingers beneath the band of her panties and she gasped and shivered at the first of his touches. She turned away from him, seeking the safety of his shoulder as she bore the exquisite sensations that he gave her, heat turning her skin pink and pleasure shortening her breaths. Oh, God, it was the most exquisite thing.

His mouth found her breast and she arched from the bed, the sound of her own pleas almost as erotic as his fingers. She was panting in need and he pulled back to watch her, his own arousal clear for her to see. Her pleasure was *his*. She understood that now. She felt that as he held her with his gaze and, completely safe in his hands, she reached higher and higher until she could barely breathe past her pleasure and then she felt him inside her, his thumb against her, but a finger deep within her, filling her nearly to how she wanted to be filled, but it was close enough to push her into nothing but sheer bliss.

Mateo had never seen anything more perfect. His pulse thundered as if it had been his own climax he'd just experienced. Sweat had beaded his brow and tipped down his back as Evie began to slowly blink her eyes open, constellations of wonder and pleasure and satisfaction and just that little bit of giddy excitement he could always sense in the background for her.

He wanted to kiss her, he wanted to touch her, he wanted to find every single one of her expressions and gaze at them in his own wonder. He had always put his partner's pleasure first, enjoying theirs as much as his own, but this was an addiction and he wanted more, he wanted to hunt her pleasure to whatever extremes it went to.

She looked for a moment as if she might try to make light of what had just happened, but as she read his intent, her gaze cleared and instead he fell deep into a connection that scared him more than he'd ever admit.

The blush on her cheeks deepened, her eyes flaring wide, and the swift inhale expanding her chest had him biting his lip to stop himself from taking her mouth with a passion that would have shocked them both. Her hands went to the clasp on his trousers, but he caught her hand.

'We can stop here, Evie.'

'Thank you,' she said, lifting her hand to press against his chest. 'But I don't want to stop,' she replied. 'Do you?' she asked in return. The dull alarm sounding in the back of his mind made him waver for barely the space of a heartbeat, but it was drowned out by a wave of desire that flooded his mind. The need to see her fall apart beneath another orgasm was like a living thing in his veins.

'No,' he replied as he nudged her hand out of the way and made quick work of removing the rest of his clothes, her eyes burning caresses into his skin he thought might scar him for life, and instinctively he knew he would walk away with the marks of their combined need imprinted on his soul.

He looked to her before returning to the bed, his chest locked in a vice as she lay back regally against the plush pillows, surrounded by a silken canopy, hundreds of little tiny lights flickering in the breeze like a meteor shower. She looked wanton and wanting and he nearly pinched himself to see if he was dreaming.

As he came back to the bed, she rose from the pillows and they met in a tangle of limbs and lips and tongues and teeth. Passion was an unstoppable force, but even then his first care was for Evie. He whispered his worship of her in kisses and touches as she made room for him between her legs. He honoured her with every moment he could, knowing that the seconds were slipping through his fingers. He hated the morning in that moment, resented the sun, and pleaded with the moon to stay in the night sky, just so he could have one more taste, one more touch.

He filled her slowly, but fully, and it hurt his heart to see home in her eyes and know that he could not be that for her. But he could give her everything in this night, so he slowly withdrew, before once again filling her, luxuriating in the feel of her wrapped tightly around him, thrilled by the cries of her pleasure-filled moans as they drew closer and closer to oblivion. Pleasure built hot step by hot step and sweat slicked their bodies. Time lost meaning as desire drenched touches, and kisses became as sensual as the glide of their hips. Their bodies danced together to a rhythm unique to that night and known only to them, until the final crescendo pushed them into a starlit moment that stretched beyond the capture of words. It was the most intensely erotic experience of Mateo's life and he knew—in that moment—no one else would ever match it.

CHAPTER NINE

STANDING AT THE bow of the yacht, Mateo watched Evie talking to Annie and the captain, explaining how long they might be gone. The captain didn't seem happy about letting the two of them go to the island alone, and his genuine concern over their safety had Mateo double- and triple-checking they had what they needed. The small speedboat was a similar make to one he'd used before, and he'd promised that safety was his absolute priority. He had stowed the small rucksack containing a satellite phone, a flare gun and emergency first-aid kits. They had both listened to the warnings about seismic and volcanic activity in the area, along with the risk of tsunamis. He had recognised, very quickly, that the captain was not exaggerating his warnings and had asked Evie, again, if they shouldn't wait.

'For what?' she'd asked.

Mateo hated that he didn't actually have an answer for that, as Evie must have predicted, because of the knowing gleam in her eye. A gleam that had turned molten when held just a little too long.

If he'd thought spending the night with Evie would have got anything out of his system, if he'd thought that he'd have been able to indulge his addiction to her just once and walk away, then he had been utterly and irrevocably wrong. He didn't know which of them had been worse, which of them had craved the other's touch more, needed the other's kiss more than their next breath, but he did know that it couldn't continue.

If Annie had noticed the red mark on Evie's neck from where his open-mouthed kiss had lingered too long and sucked too hard, she hadn't mentioned it when she came to pick them up from the island that morning. When he'd reached out for Evie, still half-asleep, her side of the bed had been cool. Without opening his eyes, he'd fisted the empty sheet in his hands and remembered the words she'd given him the night before.

Just for tonight.

They were a curse and a promise in his head.

'Are you ready?' Evie asked.

'At your service,' he replied without missing a beat, despite the bent of his thoughts. He held out his hand to her, helping her into the small speedboat.

'If you have any problems,' said the captain, 'just call in.'

Mateo nodded and pushed them away from the side of the yacht, before turning the key in the ignition and firing up the speedboat's engine. He manoeuvred the boat to face towards the island up ahead, surrounded by a series of dangerous rocky outcrops creating currents that needed some careful handling. The captain had explained that the island's layout, with its jagged and steep incline making it inhospitable for development, and the approach so tricky as to permit only one boat at a time in and out, made it unattractive for tourism. Nestled further away from the easier to access and much more pleasant islands closer to the main thoroughfares, it was rarely given a second look. The billionaires had spent their money on much easier islands, but as they approached, Mateo could still appreciate the attraction.

He flicked his gaze between their destination and where Evie sat on the bench seating, holding on to her hat, her face upturned towards the sun, looking for the world like a tourist on her way to a deserted beach. If she hadn't been wearing walking boots, canvas trousers and a loose linen shirt.

He'd been slightly disconcerted when he'd dressed in what she called her field-work clothing. Disconcerted by the shocking jolt of lust that had speared him by her efficient, utterly practical work uniform. Then again, he was beginning to fear that it might not actually matter what she was wearing, because it was her—*her*, unique, utterly spectacular, fascinatingly focused, intently determined *her*—that he was attracted to beyond reason.

'You should stop looking at me like that,' she said, her eyes still closed.

'I don't know what you're talking about,' he replied, a half-smile reluctantly pulling at his lips as

he steered the speedboat in an arc to land as close
to the small strip of beach the captain had suggested
would make the most logical place to land the boat.

The movement of the speedboat mirrored the
twists and turns of her stomach. As she hid behind
dark glasses and basked in the sun, strangely it was
Mateo's attention that grounded her. Grounded her
in something tangible rather than the hypothetical
that lay at the end of their journey.

The night before had connected them on a deeply
physical level; an awareness of him she could never
have imagined lay like a second skin over her body.
It was as if she were a sunflower turning to face
him, seeking him out, and the instinctive indepen-
dence in her chafed a little. But despite that, she was
impossibly thankful that she wasn't doing this alone
because she was suddenly nervous.

Nervous that they would find nothing. That she
wouldn't be able to validate the Professor's theories,
that she wouldn't be able to give the Queen and her
father what they wanted. What if she failed them?
What if she failed because she wasn't good enough?
She pressed a palm to her chest and took a breath,
trying to ground herself on a moving vessel.

You want to be as strong as Isabella?
How did you not know that you already are?

The words Mateo had given her the night before
whispered the strength and confidence into her soul.
Because for the first time, ever, she had seen herself through Mateo's eyes, she had seen herself as

he had—as strong and powerful as Isabella, a Pirate Princess.

And as she looked up at the uninhabited island, through the series of jagged rocks waiting to damage and break those who would trespass on its shores, she felt something unfurl in her chest. A knowing, deep and instinctive, as if she was on the brink of discovering something significant.

The island the coordinates had brought them to wasn't quite the small desert island with a palm tree and nothing but sand one imagined for a treasure hunt. Large, dark, craggy rocks loomed unwelcomingly above the sliver of white sandy beach she caught glimpses of as the speedboat surfed the tricky tides, making it appear taller than it was wide. But despite that, she was sure that they would find *something* here. Something to validate the Professor's research, to give the Queen and her father what they needed, and maybe, just maybe, even something for her.

Mateo jerked the wheel as they drew too close to one of the perilous formations dotted between them and their landing point, and Evie cringed at the thunderous sound as the side of the boat scraped against rock.

Mateo grimaced, but said nothing, clearly needing all his concentration to manoeuvre them away. His forearms corded as he yanked the wheel one way and another into the swell of the tide, pushing them back while he gently urged them forward. Not too much throttle but enough to slowly tease the boat away from the rocks.

By the time they made it through the dangerous maze of rocks and tides and to the beach, they were both damp from sea spray, a little breathless, and nearly an hour later than they had imagined arriving. With his shoes tied together by their laces and hung around his neck, Mateo rolled up his trousers, jumped over the side of the boat and pulled the speedboat to shore. He secured the boat and turned to her, holding out his hand, and for the breadth of a heartbeat Evie saw him as he'd been the night before, welcoming her to a candlelit dinner on a bleached blond beach dusted by dusk and heat in his eyes. Her body throbbed in the memory of last night—the one night she'd asked him for. Just one. She would never regret asking for what she wanted. And even though there would be no more nights like it, she would never regret what they had shared.

He called her name as if sensing she was elsewhere and, steeling herself, she took his hand and jumped down onto the sand, adjusting the straps of her rucksack and studying the GPS tracker to locate themselves in relation to the coordinates. She waited for Mateo to put his shoes back on and nod to her that he was ready.

'This is your show, Evelyn. You lead, I'll follow.'

If only he would, she thought.

An hour later of really quite difficult climbing, up a near invisible and definitely deteriorated track, they

arrived at the summit of the island. The cover provided by the thick and tangled vegetation that had
protected them from the sun gave way to a clear blue
sky that balanced on an azure horizon line from the
sea. The sun beat down on them, drying her sweat
to a salty residue around her neck.

Shading her eyes with her hand, she looked out at
the Philippine Sea, and in her heart Evie saw eighteenth-century ships sailing in the hazy distance.
The pulse pounding against her eardrums was like
explosions from a canon firing at a pirate ship, and
beneath it all was a whisper from Isabella asking her
to find her. A bead of sweat turned icy cold and fell
down her spine as Mateo pressed a flask of water
into her hands and gently tugged her into the shade.

'Drink,' he ordered.

She shook her head at the command, reluctant to
leave her thoughts.

'Evie, you need some water. You haven't had any
since we got off the boat.'

Reluctantly she caved in and went to sit next to
where Mateo was perched against a smooth jut of
rock beneath a palm casting dappled shade, taking
a mouthful of water and only then realising how
thirsty she really was.

She half expected him to press to question, or
suggest they turn back, or try and take the lead, but
he didn't. Not once. She may have been teaching in
a classroom for the last two years, but even fellow
students had overstepped her when they'd been in
the field. Whether it was her age, or her gender, she

had been pushed to the back. And yes, it was only the two of them here, but it wasn't that either. Mateo trusted her to know her limits and herself here, and that…that was something incredible to her.

And she wished it hadn't happened just when she was about to fail.

'What is it?' he asked as if sensing her feelings.

'We're here.'

'Where?'

'At the coordinates.'

And there was nothing. No building, or sign of life in the present or the past. She scanned the area again, knowing that she could happily spend days here combing every single inch of the craggy out-crop…but the sight of absolutely *nothing* shook her.

Mateo remembered his father being like this some-times. The extent of focused frustration almost a physical thing. He checked his watch, aware of the time ticking away, knowing that Evie would be feel-ing it too, so he chose his words carefully.

'What was Isabella like?'

Evie frowned up at him.

'You've studied her, you *know* her. Would she have been obvious about whatever it was she may have hidden here? Would she have placed it behind another clue?' he asked, unaware of when he had slipped from disbelief to belief that Isabella and Loriella were the same person. 'What would *you* have done?' he asked.

'Well, I wouldn't leave anything exactly where the coordinates pointed.'

Mateo smiled at the indignance in her tone. 'Okay. But there *are* coordinates and they *did* lead us here,' he observed. He considered Evie, who had begun to merge with Isabella in his mind. 'But you'd want to make it harder than that, wouldn't you?'

'Not harder. I'd want to make sure that whoever found it was the right person.'

'The right person being…?'

'Friend, not foe. And friends, they know you. They'd…know *her.*'

'And what would they know about her?' Mateo gently nudged.

'That she was Iondorran.'

'So, we're looking for something Iondorran.'

'Or something that would mean something to someone from Iondorra,' Evie concluded, her eyes once again flashing with the spark of excitement that was swiftly becoming dangerously addictive to Mateo.

She stood up from the rock and made her way back out into the sun towards the summit the coordinates had led to. Standing at the edge of the island, the sea stretched out before her, eyes closed, she looked like the captain of a ship, the wind pulling at her hair and a determination on her features he'd only seen on the deserted beach the night before.

He felt the breath she took calm him as much as her and didn't even question when she had become so known to him. And even if that thought yanked on his pulse, pulled at his heartbeat, he gave them both this moment.

Evie began slowly, as if working inch by inch, methodically scanning the land around them from one side of the island to the other. She didn't use binoculars, or her GPS tracker, she just looked with her own eyes, as Isabella once would have done. She worried her lip with her teeth, a habit Mateo wasn't sure she was even aware of, but he wanted to reassure her that she was on the right track. That she would find what she needed because he knew that she would, even if he couldn't explain it.

And when she found it, he saw it in her eyes. In the curve of her lip, in the crackle on the air between them—it was almost like magic.

'Do you know,' she asked, taking a step towards a point a little to his right, 'that clematis flowers—the national symbol of Iondorra—symbolise two things?'

'No,' he replied, standing up to follow her.

'They represent both the beauty of ingenuity and the trait of artifice. Both of which are needed for the plant's clever ability to climb around impossible-to-reach places.'

She led them back into the shade provided by the thick chaos of rich green foliage, broken up by bursts of bright white and brilliant purple flowers, clustered around thick, heavy vines.

'The other thing about the clematis is that it is most definitely not native to Indonesia.'

She reached out to thread her fingers through the fragrant vines clinging to the rock behind it and he realised that she was looking for something. No, not for something. *At* something.

'Can you get your father's notebook?' she asked him, without sparing him a glance, as she began more forcefully moving the ancient strands of Iondorra's national plant.

'Of course.' Mateo reached into the bag she had left by the rock and withdrew the notebook.

She pulled out a loose leaf of parchment, the paper older, thinner and darker than the lined notepaper. He frowned, unfamiliar with it, coming to stand to look over her shoulder as she spread out the old folds creased into the paper. It looked like a rubbing, charcoal shades marking out an outline in light and dark.

'What is it?'

'I always thought it was an old doodle, but...'

Evie held the rubbing over the detail she'd uncovered in the stone beneath the clematis vines. It matched perfectly. All along, this had been tucked away in the Professor's notebook. She'd never asked him about it and he'd never mentioned where it had come from, but Evie traced the marks carved into the stone, surprisingly smooth given the type of rocks they'd encountered so far on the island.

The marks were a crude imitation of the same stylised clematis as had been on the octant. The five petals and the single stem and leaf. Five petals... She placed her fingers and thumb on each of the petals and, holding her breath, she pushed.

She felt Mateo start behind her as the stone sank back with a puff of dust. Spanish curses mixed with her awe as the stone shifted and slid to one side. Her legs began to tremble as an entrance appeared in the side of the rock. Retrieving her flashlight, she peered into the gloom and caught sight of the top of a set of wooden steps.

She turned to find Mateo shaking his head. She could read the concern in his eyes, and she felt it too. She was eager, desperate even, but not naïve. He looked off out to the horizon and she hungrily ate up his profile. The proud brow, the stubble crossing a jaw her palm ached to feel, the perfect outline of lips that had brought her the most intense pleasure. All that she collated in a second. But what took a few more moments to process was that they didn't need words for this. She knew his thoughts as much as he knew hers. She knew he was finding arguments for them to turn back, warring with his desire to let her do this. Three days ago, he would have thrown her over his shoulder and left the island. But now? It wasn't just that he was also invested in proving his father's theories. She felt, believed, hoped, that it was also because of her. Because he trusted her. What they had shared last night, that connection, it was more than just physical, even if she tried to keep telling herself it wasn't.

'We do it safe and we do it right,' he said, when he finally levelled her with a gaze.

'Yes, we do,' she agreed.

* * *

They checked and rechecked their bags. Mateo pulled ropes, harnesses, torches, flare guns, first-aid kits and water from their bags and put them all back, while Evie stood a little way into the cave that the rock door had revealed.

She passed the torch's beam over the top of the wooden steps that led down into the maw of darkness below. Behind her she heard the snap of an emergency glowstick, and a flash of bright neon swept over her shoulder and down into the pit.

The staircase that wrapped around the inside of the narrow circular well had been protected from the elements, but that didn't mean that it hadn't deteriorated in the last two hundred and fifty years. If they were doing this properly…

'At least one of us should stay up here,' she said.

'There are only two of us,' he replied.

'I know, but—'

'Evie, I know that you're tough and I know that you're strong—maybe to your own detriment sometimes—but I'm coming with you and that doesn't diminish those things about you,' Mateo stated, and Evie tried not to let the overwhelming relief go to her head.

She was about to take the first step, when Mateo caught her arm. 'And if at any point, any, you want to turn back or you get a bad feeling…'

She bit back the innate knee-jerk reply of 'I won't', and instead replied as she should and as she felt: truthfully. 'We'll turn back. I promise.'

Evie had no idea how much time had passed. She'd been so utterly focused on her footing, on searching for signs of who had made the wooden staircase, scanning the walls for any kind of graffiti, or impressions of who had walked these steps before them.

Had Isabella walked these steps? Who had made them and where did they lead? She had never lied to Mateo…it wasn't about the treasure at all. But she really did want to find something. It was a need in her blood like…like the way she had needed Mateo the night before.

She'd been so lost in her thoughts that she didn't immediately notice when the wood of the next step creaked beneath her foot. It happened in a heartbeat that stretched over an eternity. She just dropped, every nerve ending screaming out in shock, her breath catching in her lungs as she reached out to grasp nothing, and then—

Her arm pulled tight and her body hung in midair. Mateo's grip on her hand and wrist a steel lifeline tying her to him.

'Don't look down,' he commanded and nothing in her would have refused his order. His arm bulged beneath the line of the T-shirt sleeve as he worked to pull her up. She had to reach up with her free hand, which he caught and then reached for her elbow, inch by inch dragging her out of the darkness against him until she could get her feet on the same step.

Panting and out of breath, he asked if she could get around the step below. Heart still pounding, legs shaking terribly, she quickly assessed it and nodded.

'We have to go on, I'm not sure how long the rest of the steps will hold out,' he said. Clinging to him for support she gingerly stepped around the broken wood. It was a larger step to make, and on shaking legs wasn't as easy as it should have been, but she made it and slowly, in silence and fierce concentration, they made it to the ground.

She felt Mateo's hand on her arm.

'I'm fine,' she dismissed quickly before he could ask, but her pulse hadn't yet slowed. She shone the torch around the walls, her heart thundering in her chest, but forced herself to breathe. There was something down here, she just knew it, but...

What would you do?

She took a breath, Mateo's hand on her shoulder, not holding her back but grounding her, encouraging her to think. She passed the beam more slowly over the jagged stone and saw a glint of gold. A guilder maybe? She made her way towards where she'd seen it. And gasped.

There, set back about half a foot behind a sliver of rock, was a series of bronzed cogs. It must have been used to open a door or entrance to another part of the island, because there was nothing else down here. The workmanship was exquisite, but... there was no lever. No way of making it work. She searched the cave again but there was nothing.

'May I have a look?' Mateo asked, sensing her frustration and desperation.

She nodded absently and he peered around the shard of granite that had hidden the panel of cogs.

They were incredible. Even rusted and old, they were a thing of beauty. His father would have been in his element here. Not because this might prove that he was right, but because of the human ingenuity that he'd always loved the most about history. He could see, though, that something was missing from the cogs—something to connect one half to the other. He turned his head to the side.

'Evie, do you have the octant?'

'Yes, it's in the bag,' she replied. And then, as if sensing his meaning, she hauled the bag from her backpack, retrieving the octant and passing it to him.

He turned the octant in his hands, reasoning that it was almost the perfect shape missing from the cogs. On the back of the octant, where the measuring arm met the mirror, was a tiny cog that had nothing to do with the mechanics of the navigation. It looked as if it would fit right into the...

He pressed the octant into the space and felt it slot into place with a click. He felt Evie's gasp against his cheek as she came to stand, tucked beneath his arm so that she could see. 'I think the measuring arm becomes—'

'A lever,' she finished easily and looked up at him with her excitement sparkling in her eyes like fireworks.

'Go on, then,' he encouraged with a laugh.

It was a little rusty and she strained between being gentle and firm, when just like before, there was a clunk, and a puff of air on the other side of the wall. Grinding gears sounded and they both took a step back, alarm and excitement warring in his chest.

'This is it,' she said to him, gripping his arm with strong hands. 'This is where we're going to find the answers,' she declared, and he'd never wanted to kiss anyone more.

The stone wall slid away to reveal an opening. Evie looked back to make sure he was with her and, after his nod, made her way towards it. Mateo inhaled a breath of air fresher than the stale, gritty air of the cave. Curious, he ducked into the opening behind Evie and followed the curve of the wall until it opened out and...

'*Cristo*,' was all he was capable of saying when he found himself in a giant underground cave system, so large it must have run under the entire island. But it wasn't the cavernous space that awed him, or the beam of sunlight shining down into the space and illuminating it from the cracks in what appeared to be a ceiling. It wasn't even the pool of water that lapped at a stretch of the same white sand they'd landed on.

'Is that a—?'

'Pirate ship,' Evie replied, the words coming out of her mouth on a whisper.

CHAPTER TEN

'How DID IT get in here?'

Evie shook her head, not sure. It could have been a volcano, an earthquake or even a cave-in that had surrounded a previously accessible section of the island, but it had effectively trapped an entire sailing ship here.

They walked out into the cave—a space that was easily larger than four football pitches. The light from the crack in the stalactite-covered ceiling illuminated the entire space with a gentle glow. Almost half of the space was water, lapping gently at a sliver of silver sand where the ship had beached. Beyond that, the terrain quickly became rocky, much like what they had found when they'd landed the speedboat earlier. The movement of the water suggested that it must have been coming in from under the walls of the cave somehow.

'What kind of ship is that?'

'It's a *fluyt*. A Dutch sailing ship,' she explained as she made her way towards the ship that had collapsed on its side, signs of damage from age and war clear in the ancient wood. But the name was still bold and proud and Evie couldn't help but press her fingers to her lips in shock. 'And it's not just any sailing ship, it's Loriella's.' She drew level with the ship, a shiver working its way over her skin as she reached out to touch the wood. Even in its derelict state, it still loomed upwards of nearly twenty feet above her.

'I wonder if this was once part of the island,' she said, thinking out loud, 'and an earthquake caused a landslide, or landfill or something. That could explain the sudden disappearance of Loriella and her crew.'

'But they got out? Or at least *someone* got out if the wooden steps are anything to go by,' Mateo observed.

'Someone who was able to write the coordinates down and hide them in the octant,' she stated.

Mateo nodded. 'But if they could get out, then why did Loriella and her crew simply disappear?'

'In the last skirmish, the Dutch Duke was finally forced into battle. It raged for hours, so many were killed, including the Duke himself. The bounties on their heads would have been enough to tempt anyone to turn against them, so it's assumed that they simply slipped away into anonymity after getting their revenge.'

'For going after Isabella, or killing their captain?'

'Both, I'd imagine,' Evie said, turned to look out across the cavern. Mateo beside her did the same, until she felt him stiffen. Following his line of sght, she turned towards the rocky side of the cave, surprised to find a wooden structure erected between the beach and the cavern wall. Instinctively she began to make her way towards it.

'What is that? I've never seen anything like it,' Mateo said, wonder in his voice.

Evie had a suspicion but she didn't want to voice it until she was sure. She looked at the markings that covered the doorway. Religious symbols carved into the wood with exquisite detail that would have taken much time and dedication. A sense of hallowed stillness fell over them.

She felt Mateo's gaze on her as she gently pushed against the door to the small wooden hut. Shelves lined the walls, covered in jewels, coins, old-fashioned pistols, muskets, cutlasses, chests overflowing with jewels tarnished by age and dust and sea air. But it was the two figures on a bed in the centre of the room that caught her attention the moment the door was opened. Wrapped in each other's arms, there lay the skeletal remains of Loriella Desaparecer and her lover, husband, and first mate.

'It's them,' she whispered, unaware that tears had risen to press at the corners of her eyes. She felt Mateo's hand on her shoulder, and reached up to hold it there, needing his touch in that moment.

She felt him look around the small wooden burial chamber, taking in all the treasure that lined the shelves as she had done in a heartbeat before her focus was drawn to the final resting place of Princess Isabella of Iondorra.

Mateo pointed to several lines of rough writing carved into the wood. 'What is that?'

'It looks like Iondorran,' Evie replied, leaning closer to the words above the wooden bed.

'Why would it be in Iondorran if…?'

'If this wasn't Isabella?' She looked up at him, smiling, knowing—*knowing* that everything the Professor and she had believed was true.

'Can you read it?' he asked.

'I think so,' she replied, moving just a little closer. '*"Our heart, unable to live without he who held hers, chose to stay by his side until his last breath. And then chose to join him in eternity. Long live the Pirate Queen."*' Goosebumps had broken out across her skin, as she realised what must have happened.

'You were right,' Mateo whispered and his words turned over in her heart, making her feel both elated and deeply sad for what Isabella had lost that day.

'They called her a Pirate Queen here, not a princess.'

'As a sign of their respect for her?'

Evie nodded. 'The first mate must have been injured in the last battle—the one that killed the Dutch Duke. Loriella and her crew must have come here and…' She looked at the ship, and then took a step back out into the cave, her hand pressing against her lips in shock. 'They blew the…they must have used explosives to seal in the ship and…' She looked back to Mateo staring at her. 'And she couldn't live without him, her first mate. Her husband. She…' Evie couldn't bring herself to say that the Princess had taken her own life, but Mateo must have realised, because he came to her and took her into his arms. 'Her crew,' Evie said, needing to finish the story. 'That's how much loyalty they felt for her,' Evie realised. 'They touched hardly any of the treasure and they buried her with her husband. The carving, the wooden mausoleum, that would have taken years. They would have used the wooden staircase until it was done. And no one ever betrayed them, no one ever revealed the location of the treasure for their own needs.'

A week ago, Mateo would have been surprised that anyone had managed to inspire that much loyalty, but that was before he'd met Evelyn Edwards. Somehow in his mind, Princess Isabella had merged with how he saw Evie and he could hardly separate the two. His father had looked for the missing princess for almost his entire life, and now that Mateo stood at her final resting place, he hoped that his father felt at peace.

He retrieved his phone from his pocket and swiped across the screen to get to his camera. He held it up to take some pictures, to secure the proof his father had always needed, but Evie pushed his hand down gently, shaking her head.

'Don't you want this?'

'Need and want are two different things.'

Sometimes it is enough for just one to know.

He remembered his father's words, back from when he was still a child, when he believed in pirate adventures and treasure hunts. It seemed that even though he had lost his faith in such things, he had been destined to find his way back to them.

'But this could be all you need to restore your reputation. To prove everyone who doubted you wrong,' he said, staring down into the beautiful depths of her hazel eyes that smiled sadly back at him.

'I'm not here for that. I'm here so that a king can know peace, can know what happened to his ancestor, that a queen—a daughter—can help her father, and so that a son can find his father again. That's what I'm here for, Mateo.'

Her words broke something in him, shattering something that hurt, that cost him greatly, but that he couldn't, wouldn't look at right now. He held her to him and he couldn't shake the feeling that, of all the riches and jewels in the room, what he held in that moment was more precious.

'May I have a moment?' she asked, after her breathing had settled—clearly as moved as he had been, if not more.

'Of course.'

He started to leave, when something on the shelf by the door caught his eye. The flash of a memory, his father and a painting, traipsed through his mind, and before he could question it he'd retrieved the object to take a closer look at it in the sunlit cave. But the moment he got outside, he was once again mesmerised by the impressive ship beached on the shore.

He looked around at the cave, realising that Evie

must have been right, and marvelled at how Isabella's crew had managed to bring down the rocks in such a way that the ship hadn't been damaged irrevocably. Or perhaps that hadn't even been a consideration, and just...fate.

He sat down in the white sand, staring at the clear blue water, wondering if this was perhaps one of the most beautiful places he had ever been. And for the first time in three years, maybe even more, he wished his father could be there. Without anger, or frustration or resentment, he simply wished his father could see this; the culmination of his life's work.

His father wasn't infallible, Mateo had always known that. But he hadn't understood that, as an adult and not the child he once was, it meant forgiving his father for not being infallible. Acknowledging that his father had made mistakes he bitterly regretted meant letting go of that blame and anger. But when he tried, he still felt the gnaw of heavy responsibility tightening its hold. But the unease he felt swirled around Evie. The absolute and utter shock when she'd nearly fallen through the stairs... His palm fisted instinctively. He heard Evie's footsteps in the sand behind him and buried his feelings when she sat so close to him that she could lean her head against his shoulder.

'Are you okay?' he asked her.

'A bit overwhelmed, but yes. I...' She started, staring at the way the water lapped against the beach. 'It's the culmination of so much. I wish he could have been here.'

Mateo didn't have to ask who and instead replied, honestly, 'I do too.'

'Will you tell your mother?'

He nodded. Of course he would tell her. But he feared it would cause more hurt and he'd tried so hard over the years to avoid that. And instead of seeing the sand beneath his feet he saw his mother, unable to get out of bed for days at a time, her stare into the middle distance more frightening than any of her tears. And the words she would whisper when she thought no one was looking.

I did the right thing. I did it for the right reasons.

His mother had done it for *him*.

Utterly unaware of the emotional maelstrom slowly picking up speed in his heart, Evie sighed contentedly.

'I'm so happy I saw this,' she sighed, and he gritted his teeth together to hold back the hurt so that she could be happy in her achievement.

But when she lifted her head from his shoulder, he sensed the shift in her mood.

'What is it?' he asked.

'The water,' she said, rising up to stand. He looked and it appeared that the tide was much stronger than it had been only moments before. 'I'm not sure that there should be a tide here, if—'

Whatever she was about to say was cut off as the ground beneath them seemed to groan. Alarm shot through him, and in her gaze he saw a stark fear that nearly stopped his heart. He was about to say something when the rocks cracked and screamed as the ground shook.

'Earthquake,' they said simultaneously.

They lurched to their feet, awkward as the sand shifted even where they stood. Evie went to run to the chamber, but he caught her round the waist, practically lifting her off her feet, just as a jagged crack formed in the rocks above the wooden hut.

'Evie, you can't. It's too late,' he shouted over the terrible grinding noise of rock grating against rock. She screamed as if it were her being cut open rather than the rocks, raining down and smashing the final resting place of Isabella and her husband. Mateo looked back to the opening they had come through and knew that they couldn't risk even trying to climb back out the way they had come. He looked out into the pool, the crystalline blue darkening at the back of the cave speaking to a depth he could only hope was achievable.

'Evie, can you swim?' he demanded, but she was still lost, staring between the sailing ship and the wooden hut. He shook her firmly, needing to get her to focus immediately. 'Evie!'

'Yes! Yes, I can swim,' she replied, her quick mind catching up and reaching for her pack. 'We need to find where the water is getting into the cave,' she said, speaking his exact thoughts. 'And we need to do it now. Right now.'

He nodded, glad he didn't need to prompt her further. He kicked off his shoes, thankful to see her doing the same. They stripped out of clothes they didn't need and would weigh them down, even as the stalactites hanging from the ceiling began to tremble and fall.

He cursed as they waded into the pool, fear making their movements jerky and their breaths impossibly fast. He grabbed Evie, hauling her round to face him. There was so much he wanted to say, so much that he saw in her eyes. She kissed him then. Swift, harsh, but enough. It had to be enough.

He followed after her as she ploughed through the water with strong strokes, aiming for the back of the cave. He tried to peer through the surface of the water, searching for any kind of sight of where it was coming in, of where they could possibly escape, but the water was so torn up by the earthquake there was no way of knowing.

They reached the far end of the cave and stopped to tread water.

'We have no other option,' Evie said to him.

'It will be there,' he told her with a confidence he didn't feel but knew they both needed to hear.

Together they deepened their breathing, readying their lungs to take in as much oxygen as possible, and with one last look, one last inhalation, they dived beneath the surface of the water.

What had once been a shallow, smooth pool was now awash with an unnatural tide. Peering through the murky depths, he felt salt water sting his eyes but it was the only way to find out where water was entering the cave. Just beyond his reach, Evie seemed to be heading for an area with purpose. With absolute faith, he followed her to where the rock wall arched and a blessed blue filled the darkness. With a glance back at him and his nod to her, they powered through the gap and out into the open sea, emerging from the depths with desperate gasps of air.

From outside of the cave and further back from the island, they could see the damage the quake was wreaking on the small, uninhabited island. In shock, they stared as rocks broke away from the craggy shoreline they'd stood atop only hours before, crashing down into the sea below.

They needed to swim further out. Evie drew the rucksack from her back and, treading water, searched for something inside.

'We need to get further away,' Mateo called out to her.

'Yes, but we also need this,' she said, pulling out the orange emergency flare gun, and fired into the sky. He watched it shoot upwards into an arc and, glowing a bright red, flare and spark before slowly falling back into the sea.

'Are you okay?' he demanded, resisting the urge to grab her, to hold on to her, knowing that they needed their strength.

'No. Not even remotely,' she replied truthfully. 'Are you?'

He shook his head, unable to confess that he feared he might never be the same again. He was exhausted, every limb impossibly heavy. Consciously, he knew much of that would have been adrenaline

and shock. It was a miracle that neither had been
hurt by more than scratches and scrapes as they'd
passed under the jagged rock, but he wouldn't be
okay until the captain of the yacht came to find
them. He wouldn't be okay until Evie was as far
from harm as she could physically be. And even
then, he wasn't sure he'd be okay.

Evie had stripped the wet, salty clothes from her
body and thrust herself in a shower the moment
they returned to the yacht, desperate to wash off
the fear and the sadness. Consciously she knew she
was probably in shock, not just from the earthquake
but from everything that had passed before that too;
finding the cave, finding Isabella. But also, there
was a creeping sense of wrongness between her and
Mateo since they had been rescued and she scrubbed
her skin harder and harder to try and remove that
more than the rest of it.

The captain had brought the yacht to where he
had seen the flare and found them what felt like
hours after they had emerged from the cave, but
which had probably only been minutes. He'd explained that it wasn't a particularly bad earthquake
and might not have even been felt on the main islands, but the cave would have suffered so many
tremors and quakes, it was a miracle that it was
still standing.

He'd asked them if they wanted to go back, if
there was anything left to find. Mateo's steady gaze
had held hers as she'd said 'no', letting Isabella, her

husband and their treasure finally find peace. And that was the last time she'd felt his eyes on her. Mateo wasn't ignoring her. He would answer questions, he would even smile, but he had retreated, emotionally and physically.

Even now as she looked across the cabin of the small plane that had met them from the private landing strip of the island where she and Mateo had spent the night, he felt almost a world away. She tried to tell herself that she was wrong, that she was imagining it. That after everything they'd shared, the connection between them was stronger than ever. And perhaps if she said it enough times, she'd actually start to believe it.

'We'll be landing shortly,' the flight attendant announced, and Evie felt a sense of panic.

She hadn't been able to bring her thoughts together enough for herself, let alone for the Queen of Iondorra. Everything was happening so quickly and she couldn't help but feel she was a step behind. She wanted to tell Isabella's incredible story, wanted to do the woman she'd researched for almost her entire academic career justice, because she wasn't just a figurehead to the Queen of Iondorra. She was family. And Evie knew how important knowing about family was, more than anyone.

But at the same time, Evie couldn't stop herself from thinking of Mateo.

She looked across the cabin to where he was speaking to the flight attendant. His words were lost beneath the hum of the plane's engine, but she heard the air staff offer to ask the pilot. She told herself off and instead once again tried to gather her thoughts, but they felt as scattered as sand. She reached into her bag for the Professor's notebook and remembered that she had given it back to Mateo. It was the right thing to have done, but just for a moment there it had felt as if…she had lost something so very precious to her.

The flight attendant returned and nodded to Mateo's waiting gaze. The confirmation of whatever his request had been didn't seem to make him happy though. His firm, powerful lips flattened into a line that spoke only of grim determination. And then he cast his gaze on her and inexplicably her heart dropped.

'Evelyn, when the plane lands—'

'The Queen will probably want to see us quite quickly. It will be about six in the evening when we arrive and I'm sure that she's busy—'

'Evelyn…'

'We might even have to meet her father, after all he is the one—'

'Evie.'

She didn't want to hear it. She didn't know exactly what he was going to say, but it would break her. It would break her in places she was already broken. She marvelled at that. At how, in this moment, she didn't need words or explanations, that what was being communicated to her she felt in her soul. It defied speech or language and her body was reacting more quickly than her mind. Tears pressed against the backs of her eyes. One even escaped and she hastily wiped it away, hoping that he wouldn't have seen it, but he had.

And she wished she hadn't seen the way his eyes turned from hard to soft, to hurt, to determined, all in a heartbeat.

'I'll not be at the meeting with the Queen.'

'Mateo, you have to be there. They will want to thank you for all you've done.'

'I did nothing but follow you,' he said and for a moment she believed him. Believed his words.

'Your father would want you there.'

'Don't,' he said, holding his hand up, a hint of the anger and frustration she had felt simmering in the air between them since they'd been found in the sea. 'Don't use my father against me like that.'

Shame crawled up her neck, heated her cheeks at the truth of his accusation. 'I'm sorry,' she said, regretting the words that desperation had made her use.

'After we land, I'm taking the plane back to Spain. I've already pushed back the meeting with Léi Chen too many times.'

'Is that really what's important right now?' she asked, surprised.

'Yes. It's a meeting that has been years in the making. It's very important to my company,' he tried to explain. 'It's important to me.'

Evie couldn't believe it. It wasn't that she'd expected him to suddenly drop everything, but...

It's important to me.

And she wasn't, she realised with a heart that suddenly felt as heavy as a rock.

Had she been that stupid? Again? To think that someone wanted her when they didn't? Her hand shook as she pressed her fingers against her lips.

No. She had seen the way he had looked at her. Felt the way he had made her feel. Knew that kind of feeling, that kind of *love*, had to be two-sided. It had to be.

He crossed the cabin and came to sit opposite her, leaning forward to snatch her hands into his, and even she wanted to hide from him, hide from what it was he was trying to tell her.

'Please don't make me,' she pleaded, her voice quiet and her throat thick.

'Make you what?'

'Beg,' she whispered as a hot tear rolled down her cheek, her soul aching and her heart breaking.

CHAPTER ELEVEN

THE BOTTOM DROPPED out of his world. He cursed himself to hell and back a hundred times over and even that wouldn't be enough. That he had cowed this strong, powerful, incredible woman made him feel sick.

Nausea, anger, fear, resentment, they rose up in a noxious, heady substance that choked his throat and shattered his words.

'You should never *have* to beg, Evelyn. Can't you see that?'

Another tear rolled down her cheek and he wasn't even man enough to watch it. Coward that he was, he turned away from the pain he knew he was inflicting. But it was nothing compared to the damage she could feel in the future. Damage that he didn't think he could fix this time. No amount of security or promises could heal this hurt. And that was why he couldn't stay. He couldn't.

Panic began to build in his chest. He didn't want to be here. He wanted to get out, to be away from this plane, away from her. He was angry, furious at himself for being so weak that he'd let this happen. He'd let this happen to another woman. But if he stopped this now, then perhaps it wouldn't be so bad for her. Perhaps it wouldn't be so bad for himself.

'It was just one night, Evelyn. That was what you asked for and that was all I could give you.'

Anger flashed in her eyes, an anger that covered an age-old hurt, one that he should have paid heed to, but couldn't.

'Don't dismiss what we shared,' Evie whispered.

'And don't make more of it than what it was like you do with everything else.'

'What do you mean?' she asked, paling even more though he'd thought it impossible.

'You do this over and over again, Evie. You did it with my father and with the Queen of Iondorra.'

'What are you talking about?' she reared back, but he saw it—the fear of what he was about to say.

'I'm talking about the fact that these people ruined you, Evie. They ruined your reputation. My father let you help him in his research, knowing that he could handle the backlash, but that you wouldn't. The damage done to your reputation has been almost irrevocable and he left you with absolutely no support. And the Iondorran palace?' he scoffed. 'They not only stood back and let it happen, all the while knowing how probable your theories were, they then sent you on a treasure hunt, demanding your silence and refusing to change the negative press against you. And you are so desperate for love and acceptance that you would do anything for them!'

He hadn't realised when he'd raised his voice, but the look on Evie's features horrified him as much as the damage caused by his words. If he could have cut off his own tongue, he would have. That there was truth in his accusation made it all the more painful.

'Desperate,' she whispered to herself, nodding as if considering his words, but there was a jerkiness to her movements, as if she were back in the cave, wading through water. As if the ceiling had just come down around her ears. Then the nod became a shake, slow but more and more determined. 'Not desperate, I don't think.' And this time when she looked up at him and the tear fell from the corner of her eye, she swept it away quickly and efficiently.

'But thank you for your advice. On reflection, you're right. I appreciate the reminder. Just one night.' She nodded again. 'It clearly is better that we leave this here. It wouldn't have worked. Because the one thing I know I need—as you have taken great pains to point out,' she said, the breath shuddering in her chest, 'is someone who is emotionally available. And you are not,' she said, shaking her head and twisting a knife lodged in his heart. 'You're just too much like him and the saddest thing is that you don't even see it. Which makes you doomed to repeat his mistakes. And I won't be one of those mistakes.'

'Like who?' he demanded, guilt and anger balancing on that knife's edge.

'Your father.'

'I am nothing like that man,' he spat. 'He shirked

his responsibilities...he did nothing while my mother moved us away and set up an entirely new life. I was the one who stepped up,' he said, pointing a finger at his chest, 'I was the one who made sure she was happy, that she was safe and cared for.'

'You shouldn't have had to do that, Mateo. You were a child. But you grew up burying your head in work—just like he did—so that you didn't have to confront how you felt about it. Because it's so much easier, Mateo, to lose yourself in work than to confront the painful and difficult feelings of loss and love.

'But it's worth it,' she said on a half-plea. 'It's worth it to live a full life, not a half-life of hidden feelings and buried anger. It's worth it, and *I'm* worth it, and until you see that...' she took a breath, the constellation of emotions in her eyes for once unreadable '... I don't want to see you ever again.'

Her words wounded him so deeply he was struck silent, utterly incapable of speech. It was only when Evelyn unbuckled her belt that he realised they had come in to land. She barely met the gaze that was unwillingly glued to her every movement as she stood and retrieved the briefcase she always had with her.

'Wait,' he said, the word bursting from his mouth like a bullet.

She paused as she passed by the seat he occupied, her eyes straight ahead. He reached into his pocket for the object he'd been carrying ever since they left the cave. He had always intended to give it

to her but suddenly he didn't want to, knowing that
it may very well be the last time he saw her. It sat
in the centre of his closed fist, warmed by his body
and sharp to his skin.

'When they ask for proof—'

'I don't have any proof,' she said, her words
clipped and somehow more devastating than before.

'Give them this,' he said, holding out his hand
to reveal a red gemstone surrounded by pearls, set
in a gold band.

She stared at his hand so long, he thought she
might ignore it, ignore him, but while she was staring at the ring he was staring at her, so he saw the
moment that the sob worked its way up her body. He
knew she'd recognised it, the same way he'd recognised it, from the photograph of his father standing
beside the life-sized portrait of Isabella of Iondorra,
with the ring gifted to her on her first appearance
at court proudly worn on her left hand.

It was more than proof, and more than a reminder
of his father, and more than he could put words to.
Inexplicably he wanted her to say something, he
wanted to say something. He wanted to take the
last ten minutes back, he wanted to be different.
He wanted to be the man she needed, but she was
right. He was frightened of being responsible for his
own feelings, and he had hidden his weaknesses behind hurt-filled accusations of her failings as if his
weren't so much worse. And just as he opened his
mouth to say something she plucked the ring from
his palm and took one step forward, then another,

and he realised she was walking out of his life and that he needed to let her go.

'Do you need a minute?' the Queen's assistant asked, peering at Evie in concern.

Evie almost didn't want to know what she looked like. Eyes red and blotchy, she was sure, skin an unhealthy shade of pale. Standing in the corridor just outside the private suites of the Queen and her family, she really couldn't care less. Because Mateo had just torn out her heart. But she took the chance she was offered to freshen up in the bathroom. She splashed cold water on her face and dried off with a hand towel. She just had to get through this, then she could let go. Then she could take in the way her life had just been irrevocably ripped from its roots.

Are you so desperate for love and acceptance?

Her mouth wobbled until she bit down on her bottom lip hard. She willed the tears back, knowing there would be a time to let them fall, but that now was not it. Standing up tall, shoulders back, she stared at herself in the mirror. She didn't look as bad as she felt, and that was a small mercy.

'You will do this,' she told herself. 'And then you will go home,' she said, trying not to break down on the last word. Suddenly realising that home and her life in London felt inexplicably alien to her after all that had happened.

The assistant knocked gently on the door and Evie cleared her throat. She rolled her shoulders and smiled through her hurt, all the while hold-

ing the ring Mateo had given her in her hand as if
it were her only lifeline, and she emerged from the
bathroom and went to meet the Queen of Iondorra.

It wasn't until Evie found herself before the
Queen that she realised she was in a bit of a daze.
As if half of her was here, present and answering
questions, and half of her was back in the cabin of
a small plane with Mateo, saying goodbye for ever.

'So, you're telling me that you actually found it?
I mean, found *her*.'

'Yes, Your Majesty,' Evie replied, forcing herself
to hold on to the present.

'Really?'

The Queen seemed utterly surprised, and Evie
supposed she could understand why. She'd initially
only gone to Shanghai to retrieve a family heirloom
and instead had come back with a tale so adventur-
ous and outlandish she hardly believed it herself.

In the corner of the surprisingly comfortable sitting room, the Queen's consort, Theo Tersi, was
making them all a cup of tea. Belatedly, Evie realised, that this was in her honour, and perhaps
because he and the Queen had been casting some
slightly worried glances in her direction.

'Would you like to sit down?' the Queen asked.

'Yes, that would be... Thank you,' Evie replied
eventually.

She sat at the end of a beautifully regal sofa, with
pen marks scribbled on one of the cushions and a
pile of children's books in three different languages
that almost reached the sofa arm. A little blonde-

haired girl was sprawled on the floor in the corner of the room, colouring in a design with such fierce concentration, her tongue was sticking into the side of her mouth. Her father peered over her shoulder, pride and love shining from him with an almost ferocious intensity. *This* was what she had wanted as a child, before she had realised that she would never have it with Carol and Alan. This loving, soft, easy, comfortable domesticity…this *family*. Evie paled when the Queen caught her taking in the scene as if she could read much deeper than just the basic envy that had spread across her heart.

'It has cost you greatly, this search for Isabella,' the Queen said, rather than asked.

'Yes,' Evie admitted.

'More than just your reputation.'

Evie nodded. It had cost her her heart.

Suddenly the little girl leapt up from the floor. 'Grand-père! Grand-père!' she cried, rushing to greet an old man with shockingly thick white hair and startling blue eyes. The little girl wrapped her arms around his thighs in a tight band and stared up at him with such adoration, it nearly brought a tear to Evie's eyes. Had she looked at her mother like that? Had she ever thought to look at her adoptive parents like that?

The older man, the Queen's father, placed a gentle hand on his granddaughter's head, but his eyes zeroed in on Evie.

'You found her?'

Evie nodded. 'Yes, Your Highness,' she replied.

'But I'm so sorry, the octant was lost in the cave during the earthquake.'

'Tell me everything,' he commanded.

So there, sat on the sofa, with the Queen of Iondorra on a chair with her husband standing beside her, her daughter at her feet and her father opposite on another chair, Evie told the story of how Princess Isabella became the Pirate Queen. And if she embellished just a little, to please the fancy of a wide-eyed little girl who gave gasps of shock and delight, no one in the room minded one bit. There were looks of thanks as she carefully navigated the subject of finding the remains, and frowns of concern from the adults as she told of the daring escape from the cave, but everyone cheered when she described the captain of the yacht coming to their rescue.

'I'm sorry that I wasn't able to preserve their legacy,' she concluded to the Queen's father.

Again, to her surprise, he waved her off. 'It was never about treasure, was it, my dear?' he said, looking down at the little princess, who shook her head so determinedly her pony-tail nearly came loose.

Absentmindedly her father reached down to tighten it as she replied with a big, gap-toothed smile, 'No, Grandpère.'

He fixed those piercing blue eyes on her, even though Evie knew he was talking more to the women of his family. 'I wanted my granddaughter to know that no matter what happens in life, the women of Iondorra are strong and powerful. They are survivors and warriors, who will fight for their people and their families, no matter if they are princesses, pirates, or queens. The women of *this* family? They have the power to do whatever they set their mind to, don't they, Alize?'

'Yes, Grandpère,' Alize replied with an even bigger smile, until she descended into hysterics as the once King of Iondorra tickled his granddaughter and chased her around the room until they both ran out of breath.

Queen Sofia was looking at her hands but Evie could tell that tears had gathered in her eyes, because they had gathered in her own. Sofia placed her hand over her husband's, where he had rested it on her shoulder. And when the Queen met her eyes, she understood. For just a moment, she'd had her father returned to her. A proud, powerful, eloquent man, who had fought to give something to his granddaughter, more precious than any treasure: hope and possibility.

But it was what Evie saw passing between Queen Sofia and her husband that made her realise what she wanted. It was support, it was companionship. It was *love*. And no matter how much she wanted to have that with Mateo, if he didn't, couldn't, be that for her, then it wasn't love at all.

The clench of her fingers reminded her of the last thing he had given her.

'I might not have proof that would stand up to any real investigation, but I do have this.'

She held out the ring and realised the moment they lost the King. He stared at it blankly and then

a broad smile split his features. 'A sweet. No, a...
uhm...a treat...no.'

Alize laughed, 'Silly Grandpère. But I know
where we can find some sweets,' she confided and
started to lead him from the room. Theo pressed a
kiss to his wife's head and followed his daughter out
along with the neatly dressed man in the corner who
appeared to be some kind of medical professional.

Queen Sofia sighed and set her shoulders to look
down at the ring in Evie's hand. 'I know what that
is. It's Isabella's coming-out ring. We all have one,
the women of this family.' A small laugh escaped as
if she didn't believe her own eyes. 'Thank you,' she
said, finally. 'Thank you for bringing her back to us.'

And beneath that Evie heard the unspoken words
the Queen of Iondorra intimated.

Thank you for bringing him back to us.

'You're welcome,' Evie replied, and wondered
if she would ever feel the same. Whether, perhaps,
there was a future in which she might finally try to
find her birth parents.

'Ms Edwards, I know that you are currently em-
ployed, but we have a few openings in Iondorra that
might interest you.'

Evie couldn't help but smile. Ever since she'd first
come to Iondorra she'd been taken by the beauty of
it. In her mind, somehow, it had become a country
from her very own fairy tale. But the last few days
had rocked her sense of self a little and she knew
that she needed to regroup.

Mateo really had been wrong. It wasn't that she

had been so desperate for the scraps that Iondorra had thrown her way. What had been driving her was her desire to know the past. Only, Evie was beginning to suspect it wasn't Isabella's past she wanted to know, but her own.

'I'm sure they would interest me, very much. But I think I need some time to think through my next steps,' she replied.

'Of course. Please know that if you would like to take that time here in Callier, we will provide a suite for you and open a line of credit for you too.'

'That is too kind, Your Majesty.'

'No. It really isn't. I am deeply sorry for how you were treated by your peers and regret very much that the palace wasn't—and isn't—able to change that. Yet.'

Evie held the gaze of a queen and accepted an apology that was her due. 'Thank you.'

Mateo had intended to return home. He had. He'd arranged for his car to be waiting for him when he landed and there it was on the runway, waiting for him to drive it the short distance to his villa.

He'd blocked out two days for the rescheduled meeting with Léi Chen, but this time it was Chen who'd had to cancel due to a family emergency. So, he'd got in his car and started to drive.

He was nearly three hours in when he realised his unconscious destination. He both wanted it and feared it. Feared it because of the emotions coursing through his veins. His heart hadn't beat normally since Evie had disembarked from the plane. Who was he kidding? It'd practically been arrhythmic since he'd first met her. An hour later and the muscle memory that had brought him here a thousand times had him turning off at the junction for Almería and he stopped fighting the fact that he was going to see his mother.

She was standing in the doorway, wiping her hands on a cloth when he pulled into the parking bay in front of her villa. He wondered for a moment if she'd somehow known he was coming, an instinct he previously would have dismissed, but after everything he'd seen, everything he'd discovered, he really wasn't that sure any more.

He exited the car and she opened her arms, and for the first time in what felt like forever he let his mother embrace him like a child. He was shamed by the anger and frustration that escaped from the box he'd tried to stuff them in, through the tears that pressed desperately against his eyelids, and he tried to pull away to hide them, but his mother held on tight, refusing to let go. And finally, he gave up the fight and sank into his mother's arms.

An hour later he was in the kitchen with a coffee and a plate full of crumbs, his mother refusing to hear a word until he'd eaten the sandwich he'd denied needing but had consumed in less than thirty seconds.

She looked at him knowingly and he smiled. For a moment it had reminded him of Evie. And then the knife twisted again.

'Speak and don't leave anything out.'

He didn't know where to start…there were things he'd have liked to leave out—the hurtful words he'd delivered, embarrassment and shame hot, crawling things with spikes that sank into his skin—but his mother also deserved to know that her husband's theories had not been pure fantasy, but reality.

He started at the beginning and took the slaps to the back of his head with grace, knowing they were delivered by a mother who had raised her son better than that.

There was a wistful smile on his mother's face when he finished.

'That would have meant so much to your father. That you and she were the ones to find the treasure and the proof.'

'But the world will never know.'

'The world wasn't what was important to him, Mateo. You were. I know…he…wasn't always able to show it. He didn't have a good relationship with his own parents and,' his mother paused and looked away, 'there was a lot of hurt there that was very deep. Too deep. But he loved you. And for *you* to know that he wasn't chasing fantasies, that would have been enough.'

His mother's long-ago whispered words came back to him then and he knew he couldn't hide from this any longer.

'Mama, why did we leave him?'

She looked away, trying to conceal her hurt.

'I… I heard you say that it was for me.'

Still looking away from him, she pressed her fingers against her lips. 'I'm ashamed you heard that. Ashamed and truly sorry. It was not because of you,' she said, finally turning to look at him so that he could see the truth of her words.

His breath shuddered slowly from his lungs.

'We left because, as much as I loved your father, I simply couldn't continue to live in the absence of him. It made me less; it took things away from me and I could see that it was doing the same to you. So no, we did not leave because of you. But telling myself I was leaving my husband for the sake of my child helped ease the guilt of breaking up my family. I...had no idea that you'd heard that, and I'm so deeply sorry for it.'

Something eased in Mateo's chest, but the pressure was still there. Something tapping against the walls of the emotional cage he'd put everything in for the last twenty years.

He looked at his hands, unable to look his mother in the eye. 'Am I like him?'

His stomach clenched, waiting for the gut punch he feared was coming.

Mateo's mother placed her hands over his, drawing his gaze back to hers, and the love shining in her eyes humbled him.

'You are the best bits of him and the best bits of me, *mi corazón*,' she said, the sincerity and truth of her words raising the hairs on his forearms.

'But he let us leave,' he whispered.

'Yes, he did. I think that was because he did not

know better. He did not know how to fix the problems between us.'

'I tried so hard,' Mateo said, 'to make it okay, to stop it hurting you so much.'

'I know, *mi hijo*, and it was my weakness that let you do it. Because that wasn't your responsibility, Mateo. It wasn't for you to protect me, but for us to protect you and… I don't think we did such a good job of that,' she said, the tears in her eyes hurting him as much as his own.

Mateo went to interrupt but she cut him off.

'Your father and I were always so incredibly proud of you and what you'd achieved. He loved you so much.'

'But I hadn't spoken to him for years before his death,' Mateo said, the shame almost drowning him now.

'Mateo, that didn't matter one bit. He loved you. It is that simple and that difficult,' she said on a sad smile. 'But he never blamed you.'

'How do you know?'

'Because we spoke. We would always speak on your birthday,' she said, smiling. 'You were the one thing that always brought us back together.'

This time Mateo did feel sucker-punched. All that time he'd missed and he'd never get back. The wasted opportunities because of his stubbornness, his pride…his fear.

'I don't…' he started, struggling to find the words he needed. 'I don't want to make the same mistakes as he did.'

'Good,' his mother replied, with a strength that surprised him. 'Both your father and I made mistakes—I won't let him shoulder the blame entirely. But learn from our mistakes. We turned and ran from our hurts, not realising that we could never fix things alone...but together?'

His mother let the question hang in the air as blood pumped through Mateo's veins with hope and energy and strength.

From where she was brewing another coffee by the kitchen window, his mother turned to look back at him. 'This may sound strange, *mi amor*, but I'd like to thank whoever gave me my son back.'

'Me too, Mamá. Me too.'

CHAPTER TWELVE

'Thanks, Miss Edwards.'

'You're welcome. And it's Professor,' she called with a smile after the last of her students left Lecture Room Four. She looked around the dimly lit room and wondered which poor professor they would house in here next. She'd heard that Humanities were in the doghouse at the moment, so maybe it was their turn. In the meantime, her students were to be transferred to Professor Baldick, who was, if somewhat eccentric, an incredible teacher.

Carol and Alan had handled the news surprisingly well. It had never sat happily with them that their adopted daughter was teaching at a south-east London university, and apparently any possible future plans were better than that. She had left them in their townhouse being looked after by their staff and felt that actually very little would change between them, no matter where her future lay. She would most likely continue to see them once every couple of months and, as they had little to no attachment to festive periods, Evie would be able to come and go as she pleased.

A lot had changed in the last four weeks. She'd made decisions that she'd never have imagined making the day the Queen had come to visit her here in this lecture theatre, and she'd done things she'd never dreamed of, she thought, smiling at the adventure she had taken with Mateo.

Yes, his words that last day had devastated her. She'd reeled from his rejection, questioned herself and her belief that he'd wanted more in spite of what he'd said to her, and come out of it alone. But she had survived. And that was the thing she clung to. Because even though his words had been cruel, they had forced her to confront some painful truths.

She *had* let her reputation become damaged by working with the Professor and she *had* willingly followed the Queen's request without thought to the impact it would have on her. And in some ways that showed a reckless disregard for herself which was untenable and would not continue. So now she was putting her wants and needs first. Fear had held her back for so long from too many things and she was done hiding.

She had shied away from the search for her birth parents because she feared another rejection from them. But Mateo had shown her that she was as strong and fierce as a pirate queen and nothing, not even his rejection of what they had shared that night and what they could have had in the future, could take that from her. So, she had begun to look at her adoption paperwork and was considering using her DNA to see if she had any more family out there. But that was a slow process that she wanted to think through and she felt no need to rush it. She might have lost her heart that day with Mateo on the plane, but it certainly helped her find her strength.

A strength that had been pivotal in the decision to leave USEL. Evie looked around the quiet, empty hall, a small smile curving her lips at the affection she felt towards what had been a safe place for her in the last two years. But as she had learned, safe wasn't everything. It was time to push herself, to make waves and be a little more…pirate.

It hadn't taken long after returning to London from Iondorra for her to realise that everything about her life that had once given her peace and contentment felt *lacking*. So she had handed in her notice and was using some of her savings to take some time and consider her options. While she did that, she was taking Queen Sofia up on a rather interesting proposition from a friend of hers.

And in her down time, she would work on the book that she would publish only when the Queen gave her permission to do so. Evie wasn't looking for fame or money and was in no rush, she just wanted people to know of Isabella's incredible story.

She had moved her things out of her flat and into storage, using a hotel for these last few days before she left for Iondorra. It had been a naïve attempt to avoid the Mateo-shaped figure she imagined haunting her. She'd thought, wrongly as it turned out, that if she left her flat she would no longer imagine him lingering in a doorway, or taking up space in her living room. She hoped to never again turn at a shadow in her kitchen, small and ephemeral in ways that Mateo Marin probably had never been in his life. No, leaving her flat hadn't solved anything. She would see him in hallways, corridors and on the streets, but although her mind played tricks on her, she knew in her heart that it wasn't him.

She closed the clasp on her leather briefcase and turned to find, once again, her imagination playing tricks on her. Illuminated by an open door was a figure standing at the back of the room.

She closed her eyes, holding her breath, but when she opened them again he was still there. And then, slowly, step by step, casually almost, Mateo Marin made his way towards her. It gave her the time she desperately needed, not to compose herself, but to consume the sight of him as if she were starving; hungrily and greedily. His suit jacket was open to reveal a waistcoat that hugged his torso snugly, the open-necked white shirt that indicated laziness or frustration, either of which Mateo had always worn well.

His hair, thick and carelessly tousled, made her want to feel those silken strands between her fingers and she could barely think of anything other than pressing her hand against his chest, to feel the beat of his heart, hoping to feel his own hand pressed against hers as if he'd wanted to keep her there.

She bit her lip, a sharp nip that pulled her out of the daydream.

By the time he reached her, she had pulled hurt around her like a cloak, refusing to be the same weak-willed woman she'd been the last time she had seen him. Just the memory of how she'd nearly begged him to love her cut her off at the knees. He stopped as if reading the change in her expression, his own gaze softening and offering a reflection of her hurt.

Mateo drank in the sight of her as if he were dying of thirst; great big gulps he wanted to gorge himself on. In that moment the constant sense of urgency, the anxiety driving him forward in the last four weeks, began to disappear, just from the sight of her.

He'd worried that it had been a waste of time, that he should have gone to her immediately, but he'd needed that time to get his head on straight. He'd chosen to take a sabbatical from his company. It had taken a while to convince the CFO and the board that he really did only mean six months and that it would not be for ever, but he'd had Henri's support. Henri, who was thrilled that Mateo had finally got his priorities in the right order.

Mateo had worked his fingers to the bone from the moment he'd started his company, and when most people would have stepped back after the IPO, he'd only pushed on further. He'd hidden himself, he now realised, in flings that could go no further and that wouldn't threaten the iron hold he'd had on his emotions—the iron hold he'd felt he *had* to have. All to protect himself from bearing more emotional responsibility than he could take because of the misguided belief that he had to make up for his father's mistakes and absence.

Evelyn had been, without question, absolutely right. Mateo *had* behaved exactly like his father, hiding from his fears and hurts by burying himself in his work. Too scared to confront what it was that he was hiding from. And in those last few weeks, he'd realised that he'd been hiding from himself. From the hurt that he'd never confronted at his parents' divorce. He'd found coping mechanisms that threated only to make him repeat the mistakes of the past and they no longer worked. And now he wanted more. And while those realisations had lifted so much darkness from his life, Mateo had known that there was still something missing. *Someone.*

'I missed you,' he confessed before he could engage his brain.

Her eyes flared with a hope that dimmed far too soon and it was something that he never wanted to see again, the extinguishing of that light.

Unable to help himself, he cupped her cheek and held his breath until she relented and leant into his palm. This was where he was supposed to be. He just had to hope that she felt that too. She turned so that her lips pressed against his skin, but less in a kiss and more as if to hide her thoughts or her words. He hated that, that she thought she could not be anything but honest with him. It hurt, but it was a pain he'd earned.

He slid his other hand to the side of her face so that he held her in his hands and gently drew her chin up so that her gaze met his.

'How did I get it all so wrong?' he asked her as if she had the answer.

Tears glistened in her eyes, long lashes slowly trying to blink them back, and it hurt to bear witness to the pain he'd caused, but it was also right, earned and deserved.

'I'm so sorry,' he whispered, wanting to kiss the path of the tear that fell. Content to sweep it aside with the pad of his thumb, he needed to tell her, needed for her to know how much he cherished her. How much she had shown him and given him.

'There is so much I want to say to you, but nothing is as important as my sincere and heartfelt apology. I should never have said such an awful thing to you. It came from a place of cowardice so deep and so unnatural that I lashed out in self-defence, and still that isn't an excuse.

'I belittled what we shared—not only that night, but also what we had come to mean to each other. I dismissed it and I will never stop regretting that and the hurt I caused. And more than that, I undermined your relationship with my father and your relationship with Iondorra, and I hope to God that you didn't listen to me, because I had no right and no reason to do it.

'You were a godsend to my father. I know that

without speaking to him because you gave him the support and respect that I was not able to. You were as much his family as I ever was and, no matter what my relationship with him was like, I would hate to think that I had spoiled it. Please tell me you understand that—please tell me you know what you meant to him?' Mateo half begged.

She nodded into his palm, the dampness of her tears hot on his skin but not burning nearly as much as he deserved.

'You were right, on so many levels, but the most important being that I *was* just like him. I was hiding from my feelings by burying myself in work.' He tried for a small smile.

Evie placed her hands over his, her eyes widening and her mouth beginning to open. How like her to want to deny the truth of what had happened in that moment. He shook his head slightly and pressed the pad of his thumb to her lips.

'The moment I realised what I'd done, I wanted to come back, I wanted to find you and tell you. But… I needed some time. I talked with my mother. We were finally able to speak about *papá*. For so long I had blamed myself and I would have continued to do so, if you hadn't made me realise how much it was holding me back. I…regret the last years in which I didn't speak to my father, but Evie… You gave him back to me. You healed something for me that I never thought would be healed. Our relationship wasn't perfect, and there are things I wish had been different, but you gave me a peace I never thought I'd have.'

Understanding softened her gaze, and her head dipped ever so slightly to brush her lips against his thumb, as if she was praising him with the smallest of kisses, without realising that she fanned the flames of his hope.

And finally he found the courage to say what he wanted to say, what he needed to say. 'I want you to know that I love you. That nothing you would do or say would change that. There is, and never will be, anyone I will love the way that I love you. I want all the forevers and all the happy-ever-afters with you and only you.'

Her eyes softened and she opened her mouth to speak, and when he silenced her for one last time, she glared at him but allowed him to continue. 'I'm sorry that I made you ask to be loved, so eternally sorry. But I promise you that if you give me this chance to make things right, I will show you every single day how much I love you, how you are the centre of my world and always will be. I love you. I love everything about you. I love the way that when you focus on something, it is your *entirety* in that moment, whether it is a problem to be fixed, or a new piece of information to consume, or a new experience to be had. I love that when you think things through and say it, you mean it. I love the way that you see the world differently and show me just how much there is that I'm missing out on.

'I know that you'll need time to think this out. To

poke and prod from every angle intellectually and emotionally, and I'll wait, no matter how long you need, so you take whatever time you—'

Evie crushed her lips to his, urgency and need and happiness and love all mixing together to make one heady, powerful combination. He had seen her. She knew it and felt it in her heart. For a moment she allowed herself to get irrevocably lost in his kiss, their tongues dancing together as if on their own accord, her hands at first clutching at his waist-coat, and then slipping around his torso to bring him even closer.

She ended the kiss only because she had some-thing she wanted to say, and then—hopefully—they'd be able to return to that kiss and many more.

'I'm sorry too,' she said, searching his eyes for understanding she desperately wanted. 'I was hurt and I lashed out at you. I should never have forced that on you. I was hurting but that is no excuse.'

'But you were right and I was wrong,' he argued with a sweet stubbornness.

Evie bit her lip. 'I don't think you were wrong about everything.' She smiled up at him cautiously. 'I *have* let things happen to me that I should have fought harder against. I still disagree that I let my-self be taken advantage of,' she said, shooting him a gentle glare to know that she wasn't quite happy with his choice of words, 'but I perhaps didn't push back as much as I could have. There were so many times and so many people who turned away from me, or rejected me…and that fear made me timid in ways that I am sorry for. But…you saw the strength in me in spite of that.'

'It hurts to think that you questioned it,' he said, his eyes sparking in defiance and defence. 'It hurts to think that I caused you to question it.'

She shook her head, eyes damp and cheeks aching from the smile she felt bursting from her heart.

'But you didn't. You showed me that I was strong enough to handle the things that hurt me and survive. You've given me the courage to reach for things I would never have done before. I'm beginning to look for my birth parents,' she confessed, loving the pride and delight she saw in the way he looked at her.

'I don't know what will happen, or whether I'll even manage to find them—'

'You will,' Mateo said adamantly. 'And when you do, if you want, I'll be right there with you.'

She bit her lip again, hope soaring free in her heart. 'Would you?'

'If you'd let me, absolutely. Evie…' Mateo searched her eyes for something, a sign of whatever it was he needed and finally, when she thought he'd not speak again, he dropped to one knee. 'Evelyn Edwards, you are my north star. You are my home. You are my Pirate Queen,' he whispered, sending shivers across her skin and tremors into her heart. 'Would you do me the honour of becoming the other half of my heart and life?'

Goosebumps plucked at her skin as Evie took in his words and the love shining in his eyes, but it wasn't until she looked at the ring in the box that she gasped. There, nestled in the folds of old black velvet, was a gold band, supporting a red ruby surrounded by pearls.

Isabella's ring.

'How did you—?'

'I am under strict instructions to give you this ring whether you accede to being my wife or not.'

'Accede?' Evie repeated, her smile holding back laughter.

'It felt fitting,' he replied, a sparkle in his eyes that ignited fireworks in her heart.

Evie held out a shaking hand, and Mateo removed the ring and slid it onto her finger.

'A perfect fit,' he observed in a whisper and Evie knew they were both thinking of the twists and turns that had brought them here.

He rose from the floor and took her into his arms, and between kisses he told her of how much he loved her. It wasn't until a janitor walked in on them that they finally realised that they should probably head home.

'So, it looks as if I'm house-hunting in London, then,' Mateo mused as Evie gathered her things.

'Not necessarily,' she said, turning back to him with her lip pinned by her teeth. 'I'm leaving USEL.'

'You've quit your job?' he asked, genuine shock flashing into pride. 'I'm so damn pleased,' he said, as if he was relieved.

'Really?' she asked, surprised by his reaction.

'You shouldn't be back here teaching in the worst classroom ever invented.'

'I don't think they invented—'

'Not the point, Evie,' he said affectionately. 'Do you have another job? Because wherever you're going, I'm coming too,' he informed her in that slightly, but utterly enthralling, autocratic way he had about him sometimes.

'What about your work?'

'I've taken a six-month sabbatical. I've spent too long intensely focusing on my business. Now I want to spend some time looking up.'

'At the stars?' Evie half teased.

'At you. I will never lose sight of what you mean to me, Evie. Never.' It was a promise and an oath. One that would be repeated two years later over their wedding vows. But for now, Evie welcomed the words into her heart with joy and love.

'So where are we going?' he asked as he tucked her arm under his, picked up her briefcase in his other arm and started leading her, for the last time, from Lecture Room Four.

Evie looked up at him, practically feeling the mischief and excitement rolling off her in waves. 'Well, if you're coming along, you'll have to sign an NDA.'

Mateo turned to her, surprise and something like anticipation in his gaze. 'Has another royal demanded your expertise?'

'Actually, yes,' she replied, unable to stop the smile from pulling her lips.

'How on earth did that happen?' he asked, eyes wide with shock and pleasure.

'Apparently someone reached out to Queen Sofia and she passed on my details.'

'You're a real treasure hunter!' he exclaimed, pulling his arm away as she slapped him.

'I am a Professor of Archaeology,' Evie asserted primly.

He smiled the biggest smile she'd ever seen and then whispered in her ear. 'I want to have adventures with you,' he confided, filling her heart with love.

'Good, because we're about to go on one of the best there is,' she replied, knowing he understood that she meant their lives together.

He leaned towards her and whispered, 'Okay, but can you keep the bag? Because I'm getting sexy teacher vibes and I was never a good student.'

Evie's loving laughter was the only thing she left behind her that day.

EPILOGUE

As Evie looked out at the sea of people clapping and cheering, she honestly thought she might need to pinch herself. She stood behind a small wooden podium in the back room of Olland, Iondorra's world-famous bookstore. History practically vibrated from the mahogany shelves, that familiar sense of the past providing a warmth and comfort that was the icing on the cake for Evie as she took it all in.

She had just delivered a reading from *The Pirate Queen*. The book she had written had been five years in the making and, although it had at times felt like an unending task, one that challenged and maddened, frustrated and annoyed, it had also brought her the greatest joy. She had worked closely with the Iondorran palace to ensure that the information and the history was representative but not destabilising to Sofia and her family, who had given their permission for the publication two years following on from the sad passing of the Queen's father.

She recognised the Queen's assistant in the back row, discreetly filming the event, and sent him a small smile, knowing that Sofia—a woman who had become so much a friend in the last few years—wouldn't have been able to attend without drawing attention away from what Sofia had said Evie absolutely deserved; recognition for all the work that she and Professor Marin had done.

Scanning the crowd for the faces she was looking for, she finally found them at the back, cheering the loudest and the hardest. Mateo—her husband, lover, partner and friend—had one hand tightly holding their three-year-old daughter's, and the other punching the air in victory. Isabelle's childish, happy cries reached Evie above all the other cries and applause because a mother would always hear her child, wherever and whenever she was needed. The blonde curls bounced as Mateo jiggled her and her cheers turned to laughter as they both celebrated her achievement. Their joy and support were enough to bring tears to Evie's eyes. Tears of love, of thanks, and of peace, knowing that all that she needed was right here in this room.

Carol and Alan had sent their wishes with a very large, impressive bouquet of flowers and a note, and while a part of her would always wish for just a little more than they were capable of giving, Evie also understood that it was simply that: capability. There was no intent or malice behind their emotional separation, and understanding that had changed and eased a part of her that had always hurt just a little.

Evie smoothed a hand over the twinge in her belly, their second child clearly not wanting to miss out on the celebrations. Mateo must have caught the gesture, as his eyes heated with love and pride, so attuned to her and her feelings. She could never have imagined how close they had become. Living with that kind of love and support, unconditional and unending, had been a balm she'd never expected. Before she had met Mateo, she had intellectually understood her feelings and hurts, but healing them had been done with him. And the love that they shared with their child and the child to come was a magic that she would once have called impossible.

She looked off to the side where another bouquet of flowers was waiting for her. She had read the note before the reading had started and before anyone had taken their seats. In the peaceful moment before her nerves had started—even two years of teaching hadn't managed to get rid of the stomach-churning, knee-trembling jitters—she had opened the handwritten note sent with the flowers.

To my darling, we are so very proud for you and wish we could be there with you as you prove to the world just how incredible you are. With all our love, Edward and Ellis.

She had pressed the small card to her lips and felt her heart soothed in a way that she couldn't explain. Meeting her birth parents had been one of the most terrifying and emotionally draining things she had ever done, but Mateo had been with her every single step of the way.

Evelyn had taken a DNA test a few months before she and Mateo had married in a beautiful ceremony in Spain. But even with that and the adoption papers they hadn't been able to find any information. Eventually she had conceded defeat and they had hired a private investigator who specialised in ancestry and family searches. After eighteen months of hard work and ups and downs, the investigator had led her and Mateo to Edward and Ellis. Her birth parents had been so young—barely sixteen when they had fallen pregnant with Evie. They had made the devastating decision that it would be better for everyone if they were to ensure their child went to parents who were financially able to provide the things their child needed.

Evie had expected to feel resentment; anger perhaps and loss for the things she had missed with them. But she didn't. They had stayed together and had always cherished the memory of their child. Ellis had become a surgeon and Edward had gone into technology. They had dedicated their lives to ensuring that the sacrifice they had all made was worth it. And in fact, Ellis had become pregnant with Evie's brother around the time that Evie had fallen pregnant herself with Izzy. It had created a place where they could bond, rather than harbour hurt or resentment, and together they had navigated both the past and the present in a way that Evie was grateful for.

Mateo waited for her as she slowly made her way through the crowd, people stopping her to congratulate her, others to ask if she had plans for any more books. She caught Mateo's eye, her husband having clearly heard the question, and smiled. There had been a few more adventures since their trip to Indonesia and there were certainly enough stories to tell with more books, but that was for another time.

This was the last event Evie would be doing for a while as they hunkered down as a family and awaited the arrival of Izzy's little sister. Mateo's mother had been thrilled with the news of another girl. Mateo had groaned dramatically, complaining about being outnumbered, despite the fact Evie knew he loved every single minute of it. He delighted in 'his girls', as he liked to call them, even though Henri would often claim that they were more his than Mateo's. Evie had loved Henri from the moment they'd met, realising just how much light and laughter he brought to Mateo, chasing away some of the darkness that had lessened greatly over time. Even though there were still glimpses of that determination he would get, and sometimes she would have to remind him to take a bit of time away, they had found the perfect balance. And it was all because of Professor Marin and the Pirate Queen.

* * * * *

Did His Jet-Set Nights with the Innocent
leave you craving more?

*Then make sure you don't miss
these other irresistible stories
by Pippa Roscoe!*

Snowbound with His Forbidden Princess
Stolen from Her Royal Wedding
Claimed to Save His Crown
The Wife the Spaniard Never Forgot
Expecting Her Enemy's Heir

Available now!

#4145 CHRISTMAS BABY WITH HER ULTRA-RICH BOSS
by Michelle Smart

Ice hotel manager Lena Weir's job means the world to her. So succumbing to temptation for one night with her boss, Konstantinos Siopis, was reckless—but oh-so-irresistible. Except their passion left her carrying a most unprofessional consequence... This Christmas, she's expecting the billionaire's heir!

#4146 CONTRACTED AS THE ITALIAN'S BRIDE
by Julia James

Becoming Dante Cavelli's convenient bride is the answer to waitress Connie Weston's financial troubles. For the first time, she can focus on herself, and her resulting confidence captivates Dante, leading to an attraction that may cause them to violate the terms of their on-paper union...

#4147 PREGNANT AND STOLEN BY THE TYCOON
by Maya Blake

Tech genius Genie Merchant will only sell the algorithm she's spent years perfecting to a worthy buyer. When notoriously ruthless Severino Valente makes an offer, their off-the-charts chemistry means she'll entertain it...if he'll give her the baby she wants more than anything!

#4148 TWELVE NIGHTS IN THE PRINCE'S BED
by Clare Connelly

The last thing soon-to-be king Adrastros can afford is a scandal. When photos of his forbidden tryst with Poppy Henderson are sold to the press, he must save both of their reputations...by convincing the world that their passion was the start of a festive royal romance!

#4149 THE CHRISTMAS THE GREEK CLAIMED HER
From Destitute to Diamonds
by Millie Adams

Maren Hargreave always dreamed of being a princess. When she wins a castle and a crown in a poker game, she's convinced she's found her hard-earned happily-ever-after. But she hadn't realized that in claiming her prize, she's also *marrying* intoxicating billionaire Acastus Diakos!

#4150 HIRED FOR THE BILLIONAIRE'S SECRET SON
by Joss Wood

This summer will be Olivia Cooper's last as a nanny. So she knows that she can't allow herself to get attached to single father Bo Sørenson. Her impending departure *should* make it easier to ignore the billionaire's incendiary gaze...but it only makes it harder to ignore their heat!

#4151 HIS ASSISTANT'S NEW YORK AWAKENING
by Emmy Grayson

Temporary assistant Evolet Grey has precisely the skills and experience needed to help Damon Bradford win the biggest contract in his company's history. But the innocent is also distractingly attractive and testing the iron grip the Manhattan CEO *always* has on his self-control...

#4152 THE FORBIDDEN PRINCESS HE CRAVES
by Lorraine Hall

Sent to claim Elsebet as his brother's wife, Danil Laurentius certainly didn't expect an accident to leave him stranded with the captivating princess. And as she tends to his injuries, the ever-intensifying attraction between them makes him long for the impossible... He wants to claim innocent Elsebet for himself!

YOU CAN FIND MORE INFORMATION ON UPCOMING HARLEQUIN TITLES, FREE EXCERPTS AND MORE AT HARLEQUIN.COM.

HPCNMRB0923

Get 3 FREE REWARDS!

We'll send you 2 FREE Books plus a FREE Mystery Gift.

FREE Value Over **$20**

Both the **Harlequin® Desire** and **Harlequin Presents®** series feature compelling novels filled with passion, sensuality and intriguing scandals.

YES! Please send me 2 FREE novels from the Harlequin Desire or Harlequin Presents series and my FREE gift (gift is worth about $10 retail). After receiving them, if I don't wish to receive any more books, I can return the shipping statement marked "cancel." If I don't cancel, I will receive 6 brand-new Harlequin Presents Larger-Print books every month and be billed just $6.30 each in the U.S. or $6.49 each in Canada, a savings of at least 10% off the cover price, or 3 Harlequin Desire books (2-in-1 story editions) every month and be billed just $7.83 each in the U.S. or $8.43 each in Canada, a savings of at least 12% off the cover price. It's quite a bargain! Shipping and handling is just 50¢ per book in the U.S. and $1.25 per book in Canada.* I understand that accepting the 2 free books and gift places me under no obligation to buy anything. I can always return a shipment and cancel at any time by calling the number below. The free books and gift are mine to keep no matter what I decide.

Choose one: ☐ **Harlequin Desire**
(225/326 BPA GRNA)

☐ **Harlequin Presents Larger-Print**
(176/376 BPA GRNA)

☐ **Or Try Both!**
(225/326 & 176/376 BPA GRQP)

Name (please print)

Address   Apt. #

City   State/Province   Zip/Postal Code

Email: Please check this box ☐ if you would like to receive newsletters and promotional emails from Harlequin Enterprises ULC and its affiliates. You can unsubscribe anytime.

Mail to the **Harlequin Reader Service:**
IN U.S.A.: P.O. Box 1341, Buffalo, NY 14240-8531
IN CANADA: P.O. Box 603, Fort Erie, Ontario L2A 5X3

Want to try 2 free books from another series! Call 1-800-873-8635 or visit www.ReaderService.com.

*Terms and prices subject to change without notice. Prices do not include sales taxes, which will be charged (if applicable) based on your state or country of residence. Canadian residents will be charged applicable taxes. Offer not valid in Quebec. This offer is limited to one order per household. Books received may not be as shown. Not valid for current subscribers to the Harlequin Presents or Harlequin Desire series. All orders subject to approval. Credit or debit balances in a customer's account(s) may be offset by any other outstanding balance owed by or to the customer. Please allow 4 to 6 weeks for delivery. Offer available while quantities last.

Your Privacy—Your information is being collected by Harlequin Enterprises ULC, operating as Harlequin Reader Service. For a complete summary of the information we collect, how we use this information and to whom it is disclosed, please visit our privacy notice located at corporate.harlequin.com/privacy-notice. From time to time we may also exchange your personal information with reputable third parties. If you wish to opt out of this sharing of your personal information, please visit readerservice.com/consumerschoice or call 1-800-873-8635. **Notice to California Residents**—Under California law, you have specific rights to control and access your data. For more information on these rights and how to exercise them, visit corporate.harlequin.com/california-privacy.

HDHP23

HARLEQUIN
PLUS

Try the best multimedia subscription service for romance readers like you!

Read, Watch and Play.

Experience the easiest way to get the romance content you crave.

Start your **FREE TRIAL** at
<u>www.harlequinplus.com/freetrial</u>.